"Dehumanization, although a cc
given destiny but the result of a.
violence in the oppressors, which in turn dehumanizes the
oppressed"

— Paulo Freire

Go Home!

The bangs, the flashes, screams, people running and shouting.
I am stuck, I can't move, the group of men move closer and
closer to where me and my sister are hiding. We're covered
by some baskets, I'm trying not to breathe, my sister is
shaking, I'm sure the baskets are moving as she shakes. One
of them reaches out and grabs the basket, tossing it aside
and looking down at us. His eyes are dead, there's no
emotion. He grabs my sister and pulls her up then throws her
on to the dusty floor, she looks back towards me as she falls,
I look up at him, he hits me and then it's blackness.

The fireworks keep banging but I'm not back home, I'm here
in this place, lonely and trying to make friends. I am not even
sure what all the fireworks are about, what the celebration is
for. There are kids burning dolls and pieces of wood, their
parents looking on at them laughing while they drink from
beer cans. A small boy runs up to me and smiles and hands
me a sparkler, he lights it, gives another cheeky smile and
runs away to where his friends are trying to set something on
fire. I swirl it around, watching the orange glow, I want to
throw it away but the boy keeps looking back and smiling.

When it is finished I put it on the floor, give the boy a wave and go back to my new home. I don't know how to mix with these people. They aren't bad people, but their culture, their language, it's all so different to me. I never wanted to leave home but I had no choice. They help me here, they've given me everything I need, I am grateful, but I don't want to be here. I want to be in the fields where I grew up, looking after the goats, watching my sister play in the fields, hearing my mother call us to come and eat dinner.

There isn't much in the place they've given me. There's a chair in the main room, a table that I eat on each evening and another table with a television that doesn't work on it. My room has a bed and a small cupboard that I keep my few things in. I've put a sheet over the window so people can't see in and the sun doesn't wake me up in the mornings. The bed is uncomfortable, it is too soft and I am not used to it. Each night I go to sleep I take the small picture I have of my sister from pocket and look at it, remembering the good times we had together.

I awake to banging at the door, constant knocking. I am frightened to open the door but I can't ask what they want, I understand few words and can speak even less. I open it enough so I can see out, there is a man standing there with a bright yellow jacket.

"asdjo aosjd eowr English?"

"No English"

"safdjon awerojnr oajewr money sofdoa oasdf"

"Sorry, no I speak English."

"osfoer wernjon weorjo weorj wejr wperj"

He walks away and I shut the door. I am shaking, I don't think he meant any harm but it frightened me. I am feeling sorry for myself, I have been through worse, at least it is safe here. I am going to have to learn the language, try and make things work. That's what my family would have wanted. It's a bright day, looking out the window I can see the leftovers of the party last night. It is a strange place, people all live so close to each other. There's a skinny kid kicking a ball against a wall outside, why isn't he in school? Do any of them go to school?

I should go out for the day, try and see somewhere new. I grew up seeing pictures of London in books, seeing it on the television. I dreamed of going to London and now I am here I haven't left this place that I am living in. How do I buy a ticket for the train? I don't know which direction I am supposed to go in. Big Ben, I know Big Ben, I know how to say it too, I can say it to the man at the station, he will know where I want to go. I hope I say it properly though, if I get lost I'll have a problem, I won't get lost though, I can try and ask a policeman.

I want to get up out of my chair but something is holding me back, it's like this every time I go out, like I am stuck. It feels like my mind moves forward but my body stays in the chair. This is stupid, I am in a safe place now, I have to try and make something of my life. Going out to enjoy myself will be the first step. There's still guilt, every time I want to do something fun I think of my mother, my sister, that they can't do anything fun, would they be angry at me for enjoying myself? Go! You are only torturing yourself.

At the bottom of the stairs there are three boys standing by a wall. The stairwells are dark, the light broken. They all stare at me as I walk past, I keep my head down, my eyes on the floor, shaking again. As I get past them they laugh. I hear the sound of something hitting the floor, a small copper coin. I want to look back, shout at them, tell them that really they don't scare me, that I have seen things they will never see. But I am frightened. I keep walking, I can feel their stares on my back, laughing to themselves.

"adasjn don't want aknewpq akdsn wer go home!"

I pass the little boy who I saw from the window. He looks at me, waves and smiles, I smile back, a small gesture that makes me feel safer, strange how a small boy can make me feel safe. He carries on kicking the ball against the wall, I look back, the boys that were in the stairwell are walking away, looking for someone else to bother. All of these concrete buildings so close together make me feel like I am trapped, like there's nowhere to hide. When I walk out on to the street I have escaped, a different world.

"Big Ben"

The man says nothing, he just gives me the ticket. No smile, no words just a ticket. I was so proud at getting those two words out. I had been practicing it in my head all the way to the train station. A smile would have been nice. I look at the map for the train line, trying to pretend I know what I am doing. I look at the ticket and then back at the map, trying to find what I think is the place name on the ticket and matching it with a place on the map. A man stands beside me, looking anxious, as though he has somewhere important to be. I point at the ticket and then the map, he looks at me and shakes his head, hurrying off down the stairs. I'm not important enough.

I follow him, an important man must be going towards the centre of the city. On the stairs there is a man holding out a cup, his clothes worn, a big beard and bushy hair, next to him an old dog sleeping. I take a coin from my pocket and put it into the cup, he smiles and nods his head. I show him the ticket and he stands up and walks towards a map on the wall. He points at the station I am supposed to go to, gesturing with his hands and talking but I don't know what he is saying.

"Sank you"

There are no seats on the train so I stand, looking at all the different people. People from everywhere, different colours, different languages being spoken. If only she was here with me, she loved to listen to different languages on the television, trying to guess which ones they were. She would look at pictures in magazines and point to the models, guessing which country they came from, what it would be like to live in their country. "She's Russian, it's cold there. He's American, they're all fat, that man I think is English so he must be a gentleman." I still haven't seen a gentleman.

At each station I look at the ticket and then at the name to make sure it is not mine. A big group of tourists get on the train, I must be near. They all have large cameras, laughing and joking. Am I a tourist? Will I ever be able to go home again? Or is this my new home? I envy them, they have come to enjoy themselves and then they'll go back to doing what they did before. Certainty, direction, I have none of this.

Stop! You need to start being more positive, enjoy your day, enjoy your freedom, for one day you can be like them.

It's the right station. The words are the same. I climb the stairs and as I come out from the entrance, there it is in front of me. Big Ben. The place that was in our textbooks, the place everyone wanted to go to but never thought they'd have the chance and now I am here with it right in front of me. I know I am grinning, even a small tear in my eye. There are so many people, looking up at this big clock, taking pictures, bumping into each other. I see there is a green across from it, I can go there and sit for a little while.

I find a patch where there are fewer people. I look up at the clock and then look around to see if there is anyone looking at me, nobody, there are far more interesting things here than me. I take the picture out of my pocket, turn it so that her face is pointing to the tower, hold it for a few seconds, kiss the photo and then put it back in my pocket. At least now you have seen it, it's the best I can do. I look behind me, there's a group of people eating, one of them looks away as I catch his eye, he must have been watching, I don't care though.

I am stuck again. I want to get up but I don't know where to go, I am scared that I'll get lost. This place is so big. I look around trying to find a road to walk along but I don't know where any of them go to. I see lots of people walking towards the bridge, I force myself up, cross the road and follow the crowds. I can still see the station so I can't get too lost. I stop in the middle, I wish I had a camera, people taking pictures with their families while I just stand and watch. I think it's time to go, my adventure for the day over.

In the station I take one of the small maps, take it to the ticket man and point at the place I want to go back to. He smiles and gives me my ticket. I watch the people on the platforms each time the train pulls into a stop. Worried faces, stressed faces, aggressive as they get on to the train, no thought towards the people they are barging out of the way. Am I wrong for thinking that they don't know what stress and worry is? Is it all just relative? I wish I could be like them, coming home from a job where they earn money, going home to a family.

I miss the open spaces of home, being able to look to the horizon and there being no buildings in sight. The summer evenings, when it's cool, walking down to the lake with my sister, watching her play in the water, the sounds of birds and animals. Here everything is cramped together, people everywhere, buildings everywhere, so cramped, I feel suffocated. I wish this train would go faster, I just want this journey to end, I'm breathing faster and I'm sweating. The lady standing next to me taps me on the arm and hands me a bottle of water, I swig from it, she says something I don't understand, I smile and make a thumbs up sign, I can feel her watching me concerned.

I can barely see out through all the people, I catch a glimpse of the station name, it's mine. I push through them, none giving way. Fresh air. I sit down on the bench, my breathing slows. Why am I scared of everything? Why does everything affect me so much? I can't even go out for a day without turning into a shaking mess, and now I have to go back to that apartment, sitting by myself remembering the past, trying to forget. I hope there are no fireworks tonight. I must eat too, I keep forgetting to eat.

The small boy is still there, still kicking his ball against the wall. Does he not have anywhere to go? He smiles as he sees me, kicking the ball softly towards me, I try to kick it back but miss, he laughs, I laugh with him. Laughter, something so simple can give you so much relief. He chases after the ball, picks it up and then runs towards me. He holds out his hand, I shake it and smile, he giggles as we shake hands.

"What's your name?" I understand!

"My name Ali. What is you name?"

"Michael. I live there." He says pointing at one of the buildings.

"Oh, I live there. Sorry, English, no good."

He just smiles, waves and goes back to kicking the ball. He doesn't care if I can't speak his language. The three boys I saw this morning come out of the building the boy lives in. They take no notice of me as they pass me by, they carry on towards the boy, one of them picking up his ball and kicking it on to the roof of a garage. The boy just stands there, helpless. Another one slaps him. What can I do? I walk to the boy, taking his hand, guiding him to his building. They look at me and laugh, the boy is trying not to cry but tears are starting to fall.

"What are you doing?"

"You go, no hit him."

"Go home, asdjop aosjdas oasjd asdaosdk sdljf you!"

"Go! No hit boy!"

I carry on taking the boy to his building, he looks up at me for reassurance, he's scared, I'm scared too but I rub his hair with my other hand. I feel a pain in my back, I can only see the floor, I look up and see the boy running away, I look back and the three of them are standing there laughing. I try to push myself up but it hurts, I manage to sit on the floor, my hand is cut and my back is sore. I look up at them, they turn away still laughing, one of them pretending to fall over, all of them laughing loudly. The small boy has gone.

I pick myself up, an old man walking past looks at me but says nothing. Why did I go out today at all? Walking up the stairs is painful, my hand stinging. The man in the yellow jacket is outside another flat arguing with someone. I just want to get inside, hide away underneath the covers of my bed. I lock the door, checking it three times to make sure it can't be opened. I fall onto the bed and wrap myself in the covers, my head covered, not wanting to ever leave. Why did I ever come to this place?

I cry, I can taste the salt in my mouth, the sheets are wet. I am back there again. I'm in that place that lead me to being here. That morning when we had gone out to fetch some things from the town for my mother, my sister skipping along in front of me, the two red ribbons in her hair floating about as she skipped, singing a song she had learned in school, looking back to make sure I was still behind her, smiling and laughing.

"Don't go too far ahead, the snakes will catch you!"

"No they won't! Not if you're here, you can protect me!"

We reached the town but it was quiet. All of the shops were closed, nobody on the dusty streets apart from stray dogs. She seemed unnerved, clinging to my dress. When you live with war you become used to it, you try to carry on with your life, try to ignore what is going on around you but you know when something bad is going to happen, you have to develop a sixth sense. We both knew that we should leave. It was too late, the cracking sounds began in the distance. The only place to hide was underneath those baskets.

"I'm frightened. Please don't leave me."

"I'm not going to leave you, it'll be okay, just don't make any noise."

People began to shout and the bangs and cracking sounds got louder. A woman appeared in the middle of the street screaming, looking up at the sky and then throwing herself to the floor. A crack. She crumpled to the floor and didn't move again. I put my hand around my sister's mouth to stop her from crying out, I could feel her tears running down my hand.

Men with guns appeared in the street, searching for people, shooting at nothing in particular. He lifted the basket, threw her onto the floor, his fist hitting me on the nose. When I woke up she was gone.

The noise stopped, the streets were empty. I walked back home to find it empty, the house had been trashed, belongings all over the floor, my mother and father gone, still no sign of my sister. How would I ever be able to find them? My heart told me they were all still alive, my head told me they were already dead, the only way to save myself was to flee. I took what little belongings I could, some money that was hidden, and of course the photo. I used all the money that was hidden for someone to fix for me to come here.

I have no home, this place isn't my home. I appreciate all the help, I appreciate all the kind people I have met here but it can't replace my family. Then there are those that tell you to go home. How do they know? Is it the clothes that I wear? Because I can't speak English? I don't want to be here, if I could go home I would, but I have nowhere to go. My family are gone, all I have is one photo and my memory. The photo! I reach into my pocket, it is gone. I throw the bedcovers onto the floor, searching frantically. There is little to search, it isn't here. I must have dropped it.

I can't see anyone from the window, I must go down and look for it, maybe I dropped it when they hit me. I run down the stairs and out into the space between the building I live in and the one the boy lives in. It is windy, if I dropped it it would have been blown away. I still search, looking over every bit of the floor, picking up any piece of paper or wrapper just to make sure. I look on the grass, it has gone. I want to throw myself to the floor like the woman in the town but I won't, I want to scream but I won't, it was a small thing, but it was all I had.

I am sorry Alia, I am so sorry. I've never been able to say your name since that day. Now I have to say it, I've lost the last bit of you that I had. I promised to protect you but I didn't, I don't know where you are, I don't know where mum and dad are, I can only hope that you are all alive. Every time I see a red ribbon I think of you, every time I see a child playing I think of you. I am sorry. At least you saw Big Ben. Hopefully one day you'll find me here, or I will be able to go back home and find you. No matter how much I hate it here, it can't be worse than where you are. Please forgive me...

A knock at the door. I look through the small hole in the door but I can't see anyone, I go back to the living room and sit down, another knock. This time I open the door, the little boy I helped is there. He is smiling again, he notices my eyes are red and takes a tissue from his pocket and hands it to me. I smile back at him. I can see that he is holding something behind his back, I point, his smile grows even wider. He shows me what he has in his hand. It is my photo. He says something that I don't understand. I kneel down and hug him, his face turns bright red and he runs off down the stairs, I run after him and he stops. I point at the picture.

"This Alia. Sister, one day she come."

Window

All the other kids are playing football outside on the green, I wish I could go down and play with them. Mum won't let me out, she says it's too dangerous out there, I might get taken away by a bad man. I don't want to get taken away by a bad man but I do want to go outside and play football with the other kids. How come there aren't any bad men that take them away? It isn't fair, but she never listens to me! Dad just says you need to do what your mother tells you, he never sticks up for me. All I do is go to school and look out the window.

I watch all the people outside, I know them all but they don't know me. The man that goes to the shop every evening and comes back with loads of bottles in a bag, the old man that walks his dog every night at five o'clock, the strange looking man that looks like he's a bit crazy, his hair is all funny and he can't walk properly. The kids laugh at him when he walks past but he doesn't even look at them, maybe he's scared, I'd be scared too, I'm glad that I don't look crazy. I wonder if he has any friends? He might be like me but at least he can go out for a walk.

I can see into the window of the building across from our flat. There's a woman cooking dinner, she keeps turning and shouting at someone, then she goes to the window and shouts down to one of the kids on the green. The kid looks up and then runs towards the door of the building. He looks like he's pissed off, he shouldn't be, he should know how lucky he is. The other kids carry on playing. I imagine myself down there playing with them but then I stop because it makes me feel sad because it isn't real.

The crazy man walks back past the kids but they don't look at him this time. He is wearing the same clothes he always wears: a red jumper and black tracksuit bottoms, he holds a hat in his hand but he never wears it. I don't know where he goes, I don't think he has anywhere important to go to. He stops and looks up at the window. I bend down so he can't see me, why is he looking up at me? I'm too scared to have another look. I wait for five minutes and look again. He's gone but the red cap is lying on the floor, one of the kids kicks it as they make their way home for dinner.

Should I go down and get it? Why should I go down and get it? I don't even know who he is or where he lives. He's crazy too, what if I go and get it and then he finds out and tries to find me? I can't go and get it anyway, mum won't let me out downstairs on my own. What if I sneaked out the door? Just for five minutes? She might hear me and then I would never ever be allowed out on my own. I want the red cap, I want to give it back to the man. There has to be a way I can get downstairs.

"John! I'm going out for 10 minutes, I need to get something from the shop, don't answer the door to anyone."

"Mum, my friend dropped a red hat downstairs on the way to school, can you pick it up for me so I can give it to him tomorrow?"

"What friend? What's his name? Why can't he go and pick it up himself? How do you know it's his?"

"I saw him drop it."

"He can pick it up himself, I'm not picking up things from the floor. I'll be back in 10 minutes."

The front door slams closed. 10 minutes. I can get downstairs and back again in 10 minutes. I open the door quietly to see if she has gone down in the lift. She's not there. I don't have a key though. Nobody will come in five minutes. I pull the door until it's almost closed, I hope it doesn't open again. I struggle down the stairs, going as quickly as I can, 10 flights, at the bottom I peer out the door to make sure she isn't there. She's gone. I can see the cap, I move towards it, stopping just in front. Looking up at my window it seems so far away, the building seems so big, I feel tiny.

I rush back to the door and up the stairs with the cap in my hand. If she's back she'll kill me. The door is still open, I move into my room and put the cap under my bed. Two minutes later I hear her come in the door. Please, please don't let her have seen me! She goes to the kitchen, she can't have seen me. The door bangs again, dad is home. Mum shouts at him, she says he is late and she had to go down to the shop on her own to buy some vegetables. Dad agrees with her and says sorry. Why is he so scared of her?

One more look out the window before dinner. I feel guilty, if the man comes back for his cap he won't find it. Why do I even want it? What if he dropped it on purpose because he knew I saw him looking up at me? Why would he do that? I'm not even going to be able to give it to him. If I throw it out the window to him the other kids will see and then they'll tell the kids at school that I'm friends with a crazy man. They tease me all the time anyway. I can't go downstairs and give it to him because mum will kill me, he might kill me too.

I can't believe I've lost it. How could I not even have noticed that it wasn't in my hand? I must be really going crazy, all these years of people saying I was crazy and now I really am. It's not on the floor, I'd have seen it, I don't think anyone would have picked it up, why would they want my tatty old hat? Fuck! I promised her that I would always keep hold of that hat, I've let her down. I always used to let her down and now even when she's gone I've let her down. I'm useless, completely useless, they're all right.

I'll just have to go home, passing the kids sitting on the bench I can hear them giggling and saying things as I pass them. They always do that, I am used to it, but today it hurts because whatever nasty things they are saying about me are probably right. I take one more look up to where I saw the boy in the window but there is nobody there. A carton of juice just misses my head as I turn back towards the door, splattering all over the wall. I look back towards the kids and see them running away. I look to the floor, I wish it had hit me, I deserve it.

My flat is warm, I like it. The kids can't get me in here, sometimes they knock on my door and run away but I've stopped answering it. The picture of her is on the wall, smiling down at me, I wonder if she knows? I miss it when she used to come in the door, happy and cheerful, calling my name to see if I was there. I was always there, I made sure I was indoors when she'd finished work.

"How's your day been love?"

I'd look up and smile at her and she'd smile back. She would sit down and tell me what she had been doing at work during the day, the people that had come into the shop, the funny stories she had about all of them, then she'd make us both dinner and we'd eat together while we watched television. Now that she's gone I go out for a walk each evening at the same time she'd be getting home. I can't bear to sit at home waiting for the sound of the key in the door, it won't ever come again that sound.

The hat. We went to the zoo when I was eight. All the other kids were looking at me as we walked around. I wanted to see the tigers, I was pointing at them laughing and smiling, two boys next to me were staring at me, whispering to each other and then they started to laugh. I didn't want to see the tigers anymore, I didn't want to cry but I couldn't help it. She didn't care, she just kept on smiling, walking me into the shop pointing at a red hat with a small tiger on it, I smiled again when I saw it, I wanted it and she bought it for me. It went everywhere with me, until today.

They all laugh at me around here when I walk around with it but one of them must have picked it up off the floor. I hate them, they don't understand. I'm no different to any of them, just because I walk funny, just because I can't say what I want to say, it doesn't mean I am crazy. My mind is okay, I can think, I know what I want to say, it just won't come out. They should try and be me for one day, then they would know. They couldn't do it though. They all care too much about how they look. I hate them, I wish I could tell them what I think.

That little boy at the window, I see him every day looking down at them playing football, he watches me walk past every evening. He sees what they say to me, he sees them laughing. I've never seen him laugh though. That's why I looked up at him today, I wanted to say thank you, but I can't, I thought if I just looked up he might understand. He looked scared, I didn't mean to frighten him. He knows how I feel, looking down at people that he wants to be a part of even though they tease him, he knows he never will be. He's like me, different, I know because you can just tell.

I think I'll give up my walks from tomorrow. I'll just stay in, turn the television up loud so I can't think properly, that way I won't think about hearing the sound of the key in the door. If I didn't have to eat I would never ever go out. I could just sit in here watching television or doing some of my paintings. I'm becoming more and more frightened of going out, at least when mum was here I wasn't scared, I could just ignore them, her smile was enough to make me feel safe. They wouldn't have dared to throw something at me if she was around.

It's gone and there's nothing I can do about it. Sorry, mum, I didn't mean to let you down but it's gone and I don't think I'll ever find it again. The day you left me, lying on your bed in the hospital, you said "Always keep the hat." I kept it up until today, it went everywhere, I never wore it in case someone stole it from my head, I thought it was safer in my hands. I

hope you will be able to forgive me if you know what I am
thinking. I don't think I'm going to go out anymore, it's easier
that way, please don't be angry with me.

I didn't realise that the hat had a small tiger on it. I love tigers, I've never been to the zoo though, I keep asking mum if we can go but she always says maybe in the holidays. School was okay today, the other kids left me alone, they didn't tease me at all. Some of them were talking about the crazy man and his hat. One of them was copying his walk, everyone else was laughing but I couldn't laugh too, it felt bad. If I had joined in with them they might have liked me, even asked me if I wanted to play football with them. I should have laughed.

Mum keeps saying that she wants to move, I like it here though. I know people tease me but at least I know them. I like to be able to look down at the green too, if we move somewhere else I don't know if I'll be able to do that. The lift doesn't work sometimes and she says that it's bad for my legs. I don't mind walking up the stairs, even if it does take a long time. It makes me feel like I'm the same as everyone else. I don't want to be special. I am not special, I just walk a little bit funny that's all.

There isn't anyone outside playing football today, they are probably doing something else, running and hiding in the blocks of flats trying to find each other. I know everything they do, every game they play, in my mind I am playing with them, running around, looking for places to hide, running up and down the staircases and across the landings as someone chases after me. When I see someone get caught I know I would have done it differently, I wouldn't have got caught, if they were friends with me they could listen to my advice.

It's gone five o'clock, I have the hat in my hand and the crazy man still hasn't walked past, this is the first time I haven't seen him. If he comes today I can throw it down because there's no one on the green that can see me. I have it in my hand waiting. My dinner will be ready soon, if he doesn't come I won't be able to give it back, I might never be able to give it back.

"DINNER!"

I struggle to the dinner table, my legs are sore today. Mum watches as I sit down and the pain makes my eyes close. She smiles at me, I smile back but it isn't a real smile. She looks down at her dinner, dad is eating his. Sometimes I think he's ashamed of me, like I've done something wrong. Mum looks at him, his eyes looking down at the plate as he puts the food into his mouth. She tuts and starts to eat her own food. Silence.

"Mum, when can we go to the zoo? I want to see the tigers."

She looks at my dad, he carries on eating, like he hasn't heard.

"I'll take you next week. You have a holiday from school."

"Really?!"

"Yes, I don't want you to be walking much though, you'll have to walk a lot in the zoo."

"Okay!"

Dad finishes his food and gets up, putting his plate in the sink and then going into the living room and turning the television on.

"Can I eat this in my room?"

"Yeah, go on."

She smiles but it looks like a sad smile, I feel bad for leaving her on her own. I put my plate next to the bed, I don't want to eat it but I don't know where I can put the food. There's no one outside, I could just throw it down, I pick up one of the potatoes and throw it out the window, watching as it flies through the sky and explodes on the concrete. I throw another at a tree but it misses. I only have one left, I throw it high up into the sky, it starts to fall, as I look down I see the crazy man, he looks up at the window, as our eyes meet the potato hits him on the head. I duck under the window.

I can hear people laughing, someone must have seen the potato hit him. I didn't mean for it to hit him, I didn't see him. I can't throw his hat down to him now, I don't want to see him. What if he really is crazy and he comes up here and tries to hurt me. Peeking out the window, he's still standing there but he's looking down at the floor, like a small kid that's about to cry. He turns around and drags his leg with him. There are two kids on the green laughing at him, they look up at the window and wave at me, they want me to throw another one.

There is only a piece of chicken on the plate. They are still waving at me, shouting to throw something else. The man is moving slowly, his head still down. I pick up the piece of chicken and pull my arm back ready to throw it. The kids start laughing even louder. If I throw it and it hits him, when I go to school tomorrow they will all want to be my friend. The man stops again, he holds one of his legs as though he is in pain. The kids are still waving and shouting. I can't throw it, I put the chicken back on the plate and jump onto my bed and hide under the covers. Am I a bad person?

I couldn't do it, I couldn't stay in. I kept hearing the sound of a key in my head, looking up at the door, telling myself I'm crazy, no one is going to open it. I gave up, turned the television off and went outside. On the way down in the lift an old man let me stroke his dog, he even said goodbye when he got out. Not everyone is bad. I walked along my usual route, there didn't seem to be any kids about, no one to bother me at least. I looked over the grass and in the bushes to see if there was anything red. Nothing.

I looked up at the boy's window, he was standing there. Something hit me on the head. I wanted to run but I can't run. So I just stood there looking at the ground. I couldn't move. I thought that the boy was different. I've never spoken to him, I don't know his name but I thought he was different. He isn't, he's just the same as all of them. Two other kids saw it, I don't know where they came from but they kept laughing and shouting at him to throw something again. I turned and walked away, my leg was so sore. I don't know if he threw anything, I didn't want to look back.

The kids have gone but I am still outside sitting on a bench, I need to rest. A woman walks past me and smiles, I'm sure it is the boy's mother. I want to tell her, tell her her son just threw a potato at my head, that he should know what it feels like. Nothing comes out. My anger makes me want to have one last look for the hat. I don't care if he throws things at me, one day he will be me, that's punishment for him. I push myself off the bench and struggle back along the path by the green looking for something red.

I'm going to throw the hat away. I can't give it back to him now. I know why I picked it up the other day. He's the same as me. I have bad legs, the other kids laugh at me too, I want to pretend that there is nothing wrong with me but there is. When I see them laughing at him, it's like watching myself, I don't want to be like that when I am older, everyone laughing at me, but I know how he feels. That's why I went and got the hat. It probably means nothing to him, I'll just throw it, I won't look out the window anymore.

Does he have anyone? I've never seen him with anyone. Why do I feel like this about a crazy person. I should have thrown the chicken at him. They wouldn't have cared that I have bad legs and walked funny then. Stupid man. All I had to do was throw it. If I threw it, it would have been like throwing it at myself. My legs are so sore, just for one day I wish they didn't hurt.

"John, I'm going out to see your aunt for a couple of hours, your father is in the living room."

"Okay."

I listen for the door to shut, I can still hear her footsteps echoing down the landing. He's ashamed of me. He wishes I was just like the other kids so he could take me out and not have to be embarrassed because his son has bad legs, bent and stupid looking. I pick up the chicken again and walk to the living room slowly. He's sitting there watching the television, laughing, I never see him laughing when he's with me. Why do I always blame mum? She looks after me. I throw the chicken, it hits the back of his head, I manage to get out onto the landing. I move further along to the lift, he hasn't even come out after me.

 The lift doors open and I go down, I don't know where I am going. At the bottom there is one of the kids from school waiting, he pats me on the shoulder as I walk past him, he laughs at the same time. I should feel happy but I don't. Opening the big door is an effort, I'm tired. There he is, looking at the floor, his head moving from side to side. I can't turn around quickly enough, he has seen me. His eyes look sad, not angry. Now I can see him properly he doesn't look crazy, just sad and tired. He sits down on the floor, his legs look like they have given way.

He looks up at me and points at his head, then makes some signs with his hands. He points at his mouth and waves his hands. He can't speak. He tries but nothing comes out of his mouth. He points at his legs and his face scrunches in pain, he points at mine and does the same. He knows, I think he always knew. How did he know?

"I'm sorry, I didn't mean to hurt you."

He points at his head again. I go back through the door and take the lift up to our floor. My legs don't hurt as much now, the door is still open, he hasn't even got up to shut it. The chicken is on the floor, he hasn't moved, I walk past the door and into my room, I don't really care if he sees me now. I pick up the hat from under the bed. Do I throw it down to him? Or shall I go back downstairs? I feel bad, I don't really want to see him again, I just want to give him the hat. I look out the window, he's still there sitting, there are two kids walking towards him. I have to go back.

I don't think he's going to come back, he just left without saying anything else. I have to go home but I don't have the energy left. I look up to the sky, I wish you were here, if you were here you'd help me. The day you died the only thing I had went away. I can't speak and my legs are twisted. I don't have anything else to hold on to. I thought when I showed him that we both had bad legs he'd help me, but he went.

There's a couple of kids walking towards me now, what is the point in all of this? Why did I have to be like this?

His head is still down, I walk up to him and tap his shoulder, he flinches and then looks up, I hand him the hat. I've never seen anyone smile like that before. He makes a thumbs up and there's a tear in his eye. I hold out my hand, he takes it, I can't really pull him up, I'm too small, he manages to get himself up. I point towards the block I know he lives in. I walk with him to the door, the two kids watching us, pointing and laughing. I don't care, he isn't a bad person, I know what it's like for people to not want you. Fuck them, at least we're unique.

This Time

I'm going to do it this time, I know I've said it so many times before but this time's going to be the last. I've been preparing myself all week. I'm scared, but I want to do it. If I can get past the first two days I can do it. I usually fail after about six hours. This is going to be my last trip to the off license, the last awkward walk back with a bag filled with cans and bottles. The woman behind the counter won't ever see me again, the way she looks at me with pity makes me feel ashamed, it has to be the last time. If I don't go through with it, I'm not going to have long left.

It's one of them crisp, cold December evenings. I can't feel the cold though, I've only got a light jumper on, no t-shirt underneath it. The sweat pours down my forehead, it's a sticky sweat, thick and sweet smelling, all the booze coming out of me. I've tried to cut down to make tomorrow easier but I'm going to have one last bender tonight. It ain't really a bender, not what other people would call a bender, sitting at home on your own drinking yourself to the point that you black out and will never know what you did.

I've still got that Ready Brek glow, where everything feels good with the world. I've got the confidence to look people in the eye, I'm not drunk, I just feel right, almost normal. It's a window you have, it's small and rarely lasts long but it's your connection to reality, you feel hunger, sometimes emotion, you act normally, your mind still not consumed by the madness of whatever it is you are drinking. It's a limbo, the only way out is the terror of withdrawal or the insanity of blackouts. If I could always feel like this I don't think I'd stop, wrapped in cotton wool for the rest of my life.

The grey blocks of the estate don't look as grey as they usually do, I wonder how many other people behind them windows live like I do? How many of them are contemplating the same things I am? Will they go through with it or will they fail. How many of them will make it until next year? A red light in one of the windows reminds me of being a kid and having a red lamp in my room, I don't know why I chose red, perhaps it made me feel warm as I read late into the night. Innocence, you don't know what's out there waiting for you when you're a child, everything is always going to be okay.

The woman in the shop doesn't pay any attention to me as the bell on the door rings as I open it. I need to choose wisely, it's going to be the last time. I automatically walk towards the ciders with the cheap labels on the bottles, I can smell it even though it's not open, I gag, vile stuff, but it's kept me going the last few years. I won't miss it, maybe just a small one for old time's sake, it's only a couple of quid. I hesitate as I move my hand towards the bottle to pick it up. Fuck it, I can't spend my last night drinking this shite.

I walk up to the counter with three twenty pound notes in my hand, wanting the woman to look at them, to think he's got money for once. She still ignores me, why would she care that I have £60 in my hand? I look at all the bottles behind the counter. Why do I really enjoy drinking? Is there actually anything about it that I get any pleasure from?

"A bottle of Courvoisier and a bottle of Smirnoff, please. Oh and 40 Bensons, actually make it 60."

She takes the bottles from the shelves barely acknowledging me. I give her the money and she hands back my change.

"This is the last time, you'll never see me again."

No answer, just a look of confusion. It seems she means more to me than I do to her. I'm insignificant, just another customer, someone whose face she vaguely recognises. Was I always just imagining those looks of pity? The woman who works in the off license has been a person who has been a constant in my life for years, I don't know her name, I have no idea where she lives, I can barely make any conversation with her, yet here I am feeling disappointed, illusions that there might have been some kind of connection between us shattered. Loneliness, eh?

Walking back from the shop towards my block I try to catch people's eyes, I want to tell everyone that this is the last time, that they'll never see me walking back from the shops again with bottles in a bag. They'll never see me late at night crawling up the stairs, they'll never see me shivering and shaking waiting outside a shop waiting for it to open. They won't ever see me talking to myself because I've drank so much all sanity has left me. They'll see me looking healthy, going to get a newspaper in the morning and a can of coke. They don't give a shit though.

Sitting on a bench on the green that separates two of the building blocks is an acquaintance. He'll listen to me. There's a can in his hand, holding it tightly with both hands as if it's the most precious thing in the world. He nods as I veer from my path home and head towards the bench. He shifts up the bench slightly giving me space to sit down. I can see his eyes on my bag, I know how he feels, that can is his last and he probably has no money, thinks he's won the lottery, me sitting next to him loaded up with vodka and brandy.

"Not seen you around for a bit? Where you been?"

"I went off the booze, went into some rehab for a few weeks, I couldn't take it so I walked out."

"Not managed to stay off it then?"

"What's the fucking point of giving it up? Life's shit anyway, all they did when I was in that place was talk about my childhood and all that bollocks. How's that supposed to stop me from having a drink? Fuck it anyway, I know my fate."

"I'm going off it tomorrow."

"Are you fuck. You'll last a few hours and you'll be down the off license by the afternoon."

"I've been cutting down, I'll do it this time. I've had enough of it, it's shit. What the fuck are we doing with our lives?"

"Wait until you start feeling things, you'll know how I felt then. You going to share that booze then?"

He necks his beer in one go and throws the can onto the grass, looking at my bag eagerly.

"Not today mate, it's my last little party for myself. Take this, go and get yourself something with it. Have a drink to my success too. See you around, look after yourself."

I leave him with a £10 note. He can do what he wants with it, he ain't coming to my last little party though, it's only going to be me. I wonder if, when I walk past him in the future, will I look at him with pity? Will I even acknowledge him? Maybe I'll turn into one of them people who see it as some kind of crusade to turn everyone sober. Nah, fuck that, it's about me, I don't care what anyone else gets up to. They need to solve their own problems. Time to go home and get ready for my last night of madness.

The block I live in is 10 floors high. I live on the fifth, it's a long walk up when the lift doesn't work but I run up the stairs faster than I have done in years. I haven't had a drink in a few hours now, I feel sweaty but not too bad, the bag is in my hand, it's a comfort, I know that I'll be able to have what I want whenever I want it. At the top of the stairs I stop and look out the window, looking at nothing in particular, just surveying the land. I feel a tear in my eye, is it the start of the grieving process? I wipe it away and open the door. Last time I'll be coming in here with a bag of booze.

I put the two bottles on the coffee table then sit down on the sofa. The glow is starting to fade away, I look back at the bottles, I don't really want to open them, I've never had that feeling before. It rules my life, every single thing I do is controlled by that liquid inside those bottles. I can't get up without it, I can't go anywhere unless I have enough of it to see me through the time that I'm outside. I go into the kitchen and take a glass and return to put it down next to the bottles, I'll wait, I want to show it that it has no control, that it really is the last time.

My living room is sparse, there's only my coffee table, the sofa and an old television that I bought a couple of months ago. Before that I would just sit here and drink, no television, just me, my sofa, the coffee table and a bottle. The sun is setting, the red glow in the winter sky makes me feel warm, when the next few weeks are over I'll be able to go out for walks, enjoy the sunset, enjoy all the things that I have forgotten that I enjoyed. I might even make some friends, it's not that I don't know anyone, I do, they just don't want anything to do with me.

I close my eyes for a few minutes, it's a small escape from the room, when I open them again the bottle seems to be pulling me towards it. I unscrew the lid of the vodka bottle, the cracking sound as the seal breaks, the smell of the alcohol drifting up towards my nose making me shudder. I put the lid on the table and sit back again. It's like a game, trying to convince myself that I'm stronger than I am, really I am just delaying the inevitable. I sit back up and pour the clear liquid into the glass, I pick the glass up and knock it all back in one go, it's begun, for the last time it's begun.

Half the bottle is gone and I am starting to have a fight with myself. I'm trying to convince myself that it isn't necessary to give it up tomorrow, that I can have one more little party tomorrow night. How is one more night going to hurt? It won't, surely? Anyway, when I do give it up, what am I going to do? Sit in here on my own all the time, no friends, watching shite television, going for walks on my own, what's the point in all of that? I won't enjoy it. I'll just end up lonely and bitter and with nothing to take those feelings away.

The worst thing about it all is that I'll never be able to feel like this ever again. I won't be able to feel confident, I won't be able to feel like anything is possible. Sitting here with the vodka inside me I feel like I could travel the world or find any woman I want. I can make a great life for myself, I just haven't made the effort yet, I can if I want to. I can keep it under control as well, I know I'm an alcoholic but I could just become one of them functioning alcoholics. That's got to be better than giving it all up completely.

I remember them times when I used to go down the pub and spend hours in there drinking with friends, talking about football, laughing and joking, and then we'd go off to some club somewhere or go for an Indian. We'd go back to someone's flat and carry on drinking into the morning. If I stop, give it all up them things ain't ever going to happen again. How will I be able to enjoy life? I don't think it's possible. It might be a bit fucked up sometimes but it ain't as bad as I think it is. I can see how I feel tomorrow, if I feel too rough I'll just have a drink and try again the next day, it ain't that important at the moment.

It is important though isn't it? I mean, I'm remembering all the good shit that has happened, I'm forgetting about all the bad times. All them good times were in the past, they ain't things that have happened recently. When was the last time I went down the pub? It was fucking years ago. The reason I don't go down there is because nobody talks to me, they all think I am a waste of space, a liability that they can't take anywhere. What's the chances of them changing their minds? None, they've heard it all before.

Travel the world? Find any woman I want? The only place I am going to be able to do that is here, in this room and it's all in my head. Some mornings I can barely make it to the shop, dizzy, sweating, sick, retching. Half my teeth are missing, I can't hold a conversation for long because I forget what I said at the beginning of the sentence. My brain is addled. It's all just wild fantasies that I'm using to convince myself that stopping is a bad idea. It's the same every time. I know it's all bollocks, yet I believe it because I am scared, petrified of the unknown.

More than anything I would love to go for a walk, my head held high, not paranoid because I ain't sure what I did the last time I went out. Not having to worry that people might be staring at me. I just want to go for a walk on my own to just enjoy it, the simplest of fucking things, I'll be able to stop and sit on a bench, not having to worry about how I'm going to get enough money together to get another drink, how I'm going to get through the rest of the day. Care free, that's all I want. I just want it to go away, leave me alone.

The bottle of vodka is gone, the other bottle is still sitting there. I feel unusually tired, normally I'd have the second bottle open and ready to go but my eyes are opening and closing, I'm slipping in and out of consciousness. I know that if I really am going to do it I should throw the bottle down the sink but I can't find the energy. I want to move my body forward so I can stand up but it's not responding, I'm half dreaming now. I'll throw the bottle away in the morning, it'll be a test of my resolve, a test of whether I really want to do this.

I sit up straight on the sofa, eyes still blurry, the bottle of vodka and the upturned glass is at my feet. My mouth is dry, I reach down to the glass but stop as the smell reaches my nose, I put it back down on the table. I pick up the empty bottle and walk out to the kitchen and put it in the rubbish bin. I take my only other glass and pour some water from the tap and drink it one go and then another. Back in the living room I light a cigarette and notice the other unopened bottle sitting on the table. I'll throw it away in a bit.

It's still dark outside, I turn on the television, it's six. I've slept for longer than I thought I would, usually I can only sleep for a few hours before I wake, needing to drink something. The first hour is the easy part. There's still all that booze in my body from the night before. After that first hour is when it'll all begin. The woman on the television is talking about eating healthy foods, I turn the television off again, the clock in the corner of the screen makes me feel as though time is passing too slowly, the numbers never seeming to change.

Maybe I should go for a walk? It'll pass the time quicker, it'd be good to get some fresh air before it all starts. Nah, I'm not going to go for a walk, I didn't drink that much last night, I'm starting to feel a bit sick already, if I go out and start getting really sick I'll only have one option. I feel a shiver go through my body, I hold out my hands, they are shaking slightly. The bottle on the table is starting to call me, I knew I should have thrown it away last night. Did I do it on purpose? Do I really want to go through with all this?

Two hours have gone, I've checked the television every ten minutes, I'm willing time to pass but it's going slower and slower. My hands are really shaking now, I don't want to stand up, if I stand up I feel like I'll just fall over. No one would find me, nobody would know. Everything in the room has started to take on strange shapes. The coffee table seems larger, overbearing, like it's going to smother me. When I turn on the television it feels like the people are talking to me, watching me, every word coming out of their mouths sounds loud, echoing through my head.

Fuck this, I don't think I'm going to be able to do it. It was a good idea, it was the right idea but I don't think I have the strength. Am I even worth all this? Am I actually worth having a life worth living? I curl up into a ball on the sofa, my knees against my chest, my arms squeezing my legs tightly. My hair is drenched with sweat, I can smell the alcohol seeping out of my body. I don't have the energy to have a shower, I'd fall over anyway. The bottle is on the table looking at me, willing me to open it. I can still throw it away, but I don't want to, it's my safety blanket.

I hear footsteps outside. Someone is coming to get me. What did I do last night? I wasn't that drunk, maybe I did something another night and now they're coming. The steps fade away and I breathe again. A loud bang, the next door neighbour doing something. My heart just stopped. I wait and listen out for more sounds on the landing outside but it's silent. I roll off the sofa and crawl into the corner of the room. Huddled up, protecting myself. I want to turn off the light, it's burning my eyes but I can't stand up.

The coffee table has started to change shape. It's getting bigger and bigger, taking over the whole room. I push myself back further against the wall. There's nowhere to run. More footsteps, the coffee table goes back to its normal shape. I'm covered in sweat, I relax against the wall and hold my hands out again, they are shaking uncontrollably. This is foolish, there must be another way to do this. I crawl back to the sofa and turn on the television, only a few hours have passed. I turn it off again, the colours are too much.

Just a small drop, just enough to make this a little bit easier. Surely that's the best way? Doing it like this is just torturing myself. I can just have a few glasses throughout the day and by tomorrow I'll be able to stop completely, there'll be nothing left then anyway. I lift the bottle from the table undo the seal and pull the stopper. The smell of brandy makes me shiver, it's the most beautiful thing I have every smelled. I pour it into the glass, the golden brown colour looks like liquid honey. I put the stopper back on and put the bottle back down. I hold the glass, staring at it.

I've made it a few hours. If I can make it that far I can make it another few. *You're not going to make it, just drink it, you're killing yourself for no reason, it's there in front of you, you can end it all in a few minutes.* And then what? *Then nothing, you won't feel sick, you won't be paranoid, you can get another few hours sleep.* Then I'll wake up again and go through the same thing from the beginning? *No, it'll be easier. You don't have to do it this way.* I can do it, I can make it. *You can't, you're weak, you gave up last time, you'll give up this time.* Fuck you!

I put the glass back on the table. I want to get sick, it's coming in waves and each wave is bigger and stronger, more frightening. *If you don't have a drink you are going to die, you do realise that don't you? You can't make it another hour.* Just leave me alone! Death might be better than this. *It's okay, all you have to do is pick up the glass and drink and it'll all be over.* I don't want to though, I don't want to, I just want it all to go away. *It will go away, what is wrong with you? Just pick up the fucking glass and drink!*

I pick up the glass and bottle and walk with purpose into the kitchen, I throw the glass of brandy down the sink. I pull the stopper and the smell hits me again. *Don't be stupid, this is your lifeline, anyway if you throw it away you'll only go to the shop later.* It feels as though something is holding me, my arm won't turn. *You will regret doing it, if you think the first few hours were bad, wait until the next few, you'll end up throwing yourself out the window.* I use all my energy to turn my arm, the liquid glugs out and down the sinkhole, I wait until it's empty and then turn on the tap. I slump down onto the floor next to the sink.

I'm not sure how many hours pass, I keep turning my body, running my hands through my hair, my muscles tensing, painful. I'm convinced I am going to die, at the moment, death would be a better option. I can't focus on anything, I can't think properly, all my thoughts are jumbled together into one big mess of nonsense. The only thing that isn't a mess is the picture of a bottle in my mind, it's always there. I close my eyes, feel as though I might sleep but jolt myself awake again, if I fall asleep I might never wake up.

I open my eyes, my forehead is still covered in sweat but I can focus. I lift myself up and sit against the kitchen cabinet. It's bright outside, I reach for the sink and pull myself up. The bottle isn't there anymore. I struggle into the living room, dizzy and shaky, there's glass all over the floor. I fall onto the sofa and stare out the window, the blue sky looks warm but I feel cold. I turn on the television. Fuck, a day has passed, I'm still alive. I must have broken the bottle, my hands aren't cut, maybe I was hallucinating again.

One day. I've made it one day. I still feel like shit, but not as bad as I did yesterday. My body is sore, I haven't felt pain in a long, long time but it feels good, it feels like I am existing, that I am alive. I sit up and then stand up and walk towards the window, I'm unsteady on my feet and still feel as though I will collapse at any moment. I hold the window ledge and look down to the green. That fella is sitting there holding something in his hands. I made it longer than you said I would. I fall back onto the sofa, one day, one day, one day, I've got to make it to two. Maybe when I reach seven I can go for a walk. Only six to go.

The Old Boy

Fucking alarm, I don't know why I set it, I always do it. The night before I have these grand plans where I am going to get up in the morning, go down the job centre, find a job by one, make thousands within a couple of months then fuck off to Thailand or Vietnam or someplace like that were it's hot and I don't have to worry about no one. It's like it would be so easy when you're at the end of a bottle of vodka. When the alarm rings though I don't give a shit about them plans, I just want to lob the phone out the window and try and sleep for another hour.

I can't sleep now though, I'm wide awake. I feel sick but not as sick as I'll feel later if I don't get up soon and have a couple of cans. I struggle out of bed and head to the living room to look for some dregs left over after last night. I open the door and see the window is wide open, even worse, there's red all over the walls, claret everywhere. What the fuck have I done? I can't remember if anyone come round last night. I remember being at the pub, not a lot after that. I rush round all the rooms looking for a body but there ain't one.

Some night it was last night, went back to Frank's gaff after the pub closed. Even that old fella that never talks to anyone come back as well. Right laugh he was, I didn't even think he knew how to talk, turns out he's one of the funniest people I've ever met. I had to leave after an hour, I'd had way too much, the missus went mad when I got home, I feel terrible this morning. When I left, them two were cracking open another bottle of vodka, making toasts to all the people they knew that lived round here. Madness.

He's a madman that Frank. Just before I left he was telling us how he was going to get himself a job, work for a bit and then go and live in Asia somewhere. He can hardly walk, how's he going to get himself a job? I like the guy but he don't half talk some nonsense. He needs to give up that drink as well, ain't doing him no good. I noticed his eyes were a bit yellow yesterday, that ain't a good sign, my uncle's eyes went yellow not long before he died. What can I do though? He ain't going to listen to me is he?

I sit down on the sofa, it's got to be blood, what else can it be? The wall is covered in it, what the fuck am I going to do? If I've killed someone how comes they ain't here in the house. I don't get violent when I'm drunk. Oh fuck what have I done? I pick up the vodka bottle from the floor and drink the last couple of drops, gagging then rushing to the toilet to throw it all back up. I rest my head on the bowl, sweat pouring out of me, this is madness. I hear movement at the door, I shiver, my whole body shaking, it's like I can see myself. It's only the postman.

Where did I go yesterday? I went to the shop in the morning and bought a few cans of that strong lager, went home and watched a couple of films, then I went down the pub. I can't remember who I met. I know I was drinking with that old geezer that don't say anything for a couple of hours, he bought me a few drinks. Strange old geezer, I can't have brought him back here and offed him can I? He'd still be here, what if I got rid of the body when I was in a black out? I've gotta go down the pub and see if he's there.

I had an uncle, he died a few years back, Frank reminds me of him. He used to drink a lot, then he slowly started going mad, reckoned aliens come and visited him one night. You couldn't have a proper conversation with him either, he used to forget what he was saying half way through a sentence and just stop talking. Poor fella. There weren't anything we could do though, he wouldn't listen to no one. I'd go round and see him, I'd even go out and buy his drink for him, better me because when he went out he'd shout at people. That's the way Frank's going. He'll end up like him.

I care a bit too much about people that don't really care about me, do you know what I mean? I've got a soft heart, I hate to see people suffering. Then they take the piss with me a bit, ask for money and that but I still lend it to them. I don't even think Frank sees me as he's mate, I think I'm just some geezer that he went to school with and drinks with. I've noticed that, my uncle too, they don't really have friends, alcoholics, they're just people that they know, get drunk with and then look for a few quid off when they're skint.

I think I've killed someone. Fuck this, what am I supposed to do? I need a drink but there isn't anything left in the house, that means I've got to go out, the old bill could be waiting for me out there. I pick up my old jumper that's lying on the floor and throw it on, hands still shaking, I can't see properly, everything just seems blurred and not real. I take another look at the living room, just to check I ain't going mad, it's still there, big red marks all over the wallpaper, some on the floor too. This really ain't good.

I open the door and look both ways, there's some woman that lives a few doors down smoking a cigarette on the balcony, she turns and looks at me, throws away the unfinished cigarette and hurries inside her own flat. That's not good, maybe she's gone to phone the police. I run down the stairs and over the green, I need to get off the estate, find a shop that's a bit further away, where nobody knows me. I'm starting to feel sick, I want to throw up again but I am trying to hold it in. At the bottom of one of the other blocks there's a police car but there's no one in it, I put my head down and walk faster.

I just seen Frank walking across the green, proper shifty, like he was up to something. I don't know what goes through that geezer's head. I tried to call out to him but he mustn't have heard me. There's loads of police around this morning, I ain't sure what's happening, I'll have to ask the geezer in the newsagents if he knows, he knows everything. I can't be bothered with going into work this afternoon, I never should have gone out last night. I wonder how that old geezer is this morning? Probably waiting for the pub to open, last night was the first time I'd seen him out of it.

Looks like the police are going around knocking on people's doors. Something bad must have happened, they don't usually do that. Frank must have got really pissed and killed the old man, ha ha! Na, he wouldn't have done something like that, never seen him get violent before. I should go and give him a knock before I go home, make sure he's okay, I feel a bit responsible for him, knew him since we were kids. I know he's an alcoholic and all that, but he's my mate, I don't want nothing bad happening to him.

I look up at the cameras in the shop, I don't think they work. The shopkeeper looks at me with suspicion, well I think it's suspicion, another geezer comes out of the back of the shop and pretends to stack some shelves next to me while I look through the shelves of booze. The cameras must work. I see what I want, a bottle of cheap cider, £1 for a litre and a half, it tastes like drinking chemicals mixed with gone off apples, needs must and all that, I could really do with a bottle of vodka but I didn't bring enough money out and I can't go back.

"Anything else sir?"

"Yeah, 10 Mayfairs as well please mate and a packet of Rizla."

"You hear about man that get killed yesterday? Found his body this morning, in woods near estate over the green."

Oh fuck.

"Nah, I ain't heard about that. What happened?"

"Don't know, policeman came in this morning, said old man got killed. Probably them kids tried to rob him, went bad. Everything bad around here these days."

"Old man?"

"Yes, old man."

"Terrible. Thank you mate."

"Goodbye sir"

This is bad, really fucking bad. I've killed the old geezer and dumped his body in the woods, no wonder there was claret all over the walls this morning. I need to hide somewhere for a bit while I work out what to do, I don't want to have to go to jail for the rest of my life. I'll go down the canal for a bit and hide, they ain't going to look down there I don't think. I need to get this bottle of cider down me before I can think straight anyway. I swear the geezer that owned the shop just picked up his phone as I left.

Fucking hell, it's a right bad turn out this, apparently some old man's been found in the woods. Not sure if he's been murdered or what. It's a bit rough around here but murder is a bit much. Probably some old fella that got pissed and then fell over on his way home, tried to take a short cut. Poor fella, what a way to go. I just said to the wife that's the sort of thing that will happen to Frank one day. She don't really like Frank, reckons he's a bad influence on me. She just looked at me and said maybe it would be for the best. I hate it when she says things like that.

I go and have a fag on the balcony, she don't like me smoking inside. I wonder who this geezer that's dead is. Surely it can't be that old fella, I reckon Frank would've walked him home even if he was pissed. He might even have left him to sleep on his sofa. There was that one time I was in his house though, never seen him so drunk, he said I'd taken the bacon out of his fridge and was going to take it home for my dinner. Why would I take his bacon? Anyway, he pulled a knife on me, said he was going to cut me. I forgot about that. Nah, surely he wouldn't have murdered an old man? He did look a bit shifty this morning though.

If I haven't killed that old geezer I am going to turn my life around. I'm going to give it all up, no more booze, no more smoking. Live a nice sober life, get a job, go to work, take myself on holiday, I could have a few beers on holiday I suppose. I've been wasting my life, all I've done for the last twenty years is drink my life away and I ain't got nothing to show for it, except for maybe a murder. Always wanted to be famous and in the papers when I was a kid. Not like this though. This is a bit too much. I promise, I'll do it, please don't let me have killed someone.

I don't know where to go next, I can't keep sitting down here by the canal. I need to find out what's happened. I ain't ready yet though, I ain't ready to get put away. Fuck it I'll go to me sisters, I haven't been to see her in years, if I'm going to prison I need to make my peace with her though, we had an argument about something stupid and ain't spoke to each other since. I need someone that'll come and visit me in jail, I can't think of anyone else that would want to come and see me. I can go inside her house and think a bit too, buy myself some time.

"Excuse me sir, did you see anything suspicious last night?"

"No, I went round my mate's house and went straight home, I was well pissed, I wouldn't really remember. What's happened anyway?"

"Some old boy been murdered in the woods. Someone seen him coming out of that block of flats over there about two o'clock, he was drunk. We're trying to find out what happened next."

"Definitely murdered, yeah?"

"Someone hit him, we're still trying to find out what happened."

"Do you know who he is?"

"Nope, he didn't have I.D on him and no one's been reported missing."

Fuck. That old geezer used to live on his own, he lives in one of them blocks on the other side of the green but I ain't sure which one it is. I'd better go and see if he's in the pub, he'd be there by now, he's always there when the place opens. Fucking hell, I'm starting to think Frank's murdered him. I told him he needed to give up the booze, something like this was going to happen one day. The wife was right, there's something wrong in his head. Thinking about it, what if the old geezer hadn't been at Frank's last night? He might've done me in!

"I ain't got any money to lend you Frank, I'm skint, I can just about afford to feed the kids I ain't giving you money to go and get pissed."

"Nah, I ain't come here looking for money, I just come here to see you, just popped in, ain't seen you in a while, was wondering how you was."

"Frank, you don't leave that estate unless you're sitting with them old tramps down by the canal drinking. I'm not an idiot."

"Come on, I'm being honest, I've just come round to see ya! Just let me in for half an hour."

"You look like you've been sleeping on the streets and you stink of booze. Go on, half an hour but I ain't giving you no money."

Can't blame her really, I wouldn't let myself in. Her flat is nice and tidy, all the kids must be at school. My eyes go straight to her drinks cabinet. She sees me looking and then walks over and opens a bottle of vodka and pours it into a glass and gives it to me. I knock it back in one go, she keeps looking at me with contempt, she don't want me here, I don't really want to be here either but I ain't got much choice. I sit down on the sofa, she stays standing up, like she wants to make me as uncomfortable as possible.

"How you been then?"

"I'm okay, kids are doing well at school, job's okay even if it means I don't see the kids as much as I want but it's something you've gotta do, not sure you'd understand that."

"Look, I ain't here for a row. Did you hear someone got killed down the estate?"

"Yeah, it was on the news this morning. Some old man, poor fella, shouldn't have been out late at night."

"Did they say if they caught anyone?"

"Nah, said they're still looking for information. I saw your mate the other day, that one you used to go school with. Nice fella."

"Oh yeah, went out for a few drinks with him last night. He ain't really a mate, just someone to have a few drinks with now and again."

"What do you want Frank?"

"I told you, I don't want nothing! Listen, I'm gonna try and sort myself out, get off the drink, get a job and all that. Would be nice if you could give me a bit of support."

"I ain't giving you no money, do you think I'm stupid?"

"Nah, I mean if I get off it, can I come round and see the kids, see you, I know I've been an idiot, I know a lot of the time I ain't a nice person. I want to change that."

"You've said this all before Frank. If you stay off the drink for three months, you can come round each Sunday for dinner and then we'll take it from there. You're my brother Frank but I ain't got a fucking clue how to help you and I'm sick and tired of you letting me down. Sort yourself out and then we'll see. I've got to go to work, you'd better go."

"Can I have one more drink?"

"That's a good start. Go on, I'm going to have a shower, let yourself out."

He ain't in the pub, something's wrong if he ain't there. This really ain't looking too good. I knew Frank was up to something when I saw him this morning. Maybe I should go to the police and tell them that I think I might know something. Do I know anything though? I mean I don't know that Frank's killed someone, the dead person might not even be the old boy. Fucking hell, I don't need all this, I'm supposed to be at work in an hour and I could be doing without it. I'd better go round Frank's, I'm gonna go home and get a knife first though, just in case he tries to murder me too.

I've taken one of them meat cleavers and put it down my trousers but it keeps slipping down. All these police about and I keep trying to stop a meat cleaver falling out my trousers. I look in his window but there don't look like there's anyone there. I bang on the door a few times and shout his name. He ain't in. He must have done a runner, where would he go? He ain't got any money. There's a woman smoking a cigarette watching me bang on the door.

"Your boyfriend went out this morning, ain't seen him come back since."

"What you on about? He ain't my boyfriend. He's my mate."

"It's okay love, I'm open minded. I won't tell no one, you can do better than him though."

"He's my mate, do you know where he went?"

"How would I know, I've never spoken to him in my life. There's something falling out the bottom of your trousers."

I'd better go and face the music. I've taken the bottle of vodka from my sister's, she won't mind, she don't drink herself anyway, what's she need it for? I've killed someone, I might as well get hammered before I get arrested. I fish through my pockets and find enough to get the bus back, getting the bus back would be quicker though won't it? Nah, that's a bad idea, I need to take my time, enjoy my last bit of freedom. I'll have a couple of drinks for the old boy as well, he won't be having too many where he's gone. I wonder if he's talked to God yet?

I wonder what it's going to be like in jail? I ain't sure if I'm cut out for all of that. Once they arrest me I'm going to have to detox as well, go through the DTs, if they don't give me any meds I'm going to be bang in trouble. What if I just go on the run? That'll be easier won't it? I could just live on the streets, no one will know who I am then. You know what, that might be the best idea, I'll go home, see if there's anyone sniffing about the flat, get some money and then jump on a bus up north somewhere and live on the streets. Fuck jail, I don't think I'd be able to take it.

Boyfriend? What's the matter with these people? If he's done a runner I ain't sure what to do. I know he's got a sister, nice girl, but she won't take him in. People would have seen me leave the pub with them last night, someone might go to the police and say I'm involved, they might even think it was me. All I've tried to do is be a friend to some pisshead that I went to school with and now I might end up doing bird for murder. What am I going to do? I need to get rid of this fucking cleaver first, if the old bill catch me with that I am right in the shit.

The wife has gone out so I'm okay, I slip the cleaver back in the drawer and go and sit down in the living room. I think I'd better phone the police and tell them what I think's happened. Last night we was all singing and dancing in his room and now he's run away and the old boy is dead. Maybe he ain't done anything though. What if it's all just one big mistake? He might have just gone out for a walk for a few hours, the dead fella might not even be the old geezer, he might have just had a lie in after a heavy night. Nah, I ain't sure, I reckon he's murdered him and I ain't getting in trouble for that.

I was just thinking there, Rob come round with the old boy last night, I'm sure he did. I swear he left the pub with us. He might have done him in, he nicked my fucking sausages that time he come round my house, who's to say he ain't capable of murdering someone? Yeah, it weren't me, I bet it was Rob, I've always thought he was a bit snide, the type that'd take advantage. He knocked me out, then had a fight with the old geezer. All the vodka's gone, I've done that bottle quick, I can really feel it now. Ain't no way I've killed someone, it was that Rob.

I'll just go to the old bill and tell them that I remember everything, Rob hit me and then I watched him do the old man in and carry the body off, must have dumped it in the woods to make it look like a robbery. Well this is good, I don't have to go jail now, or run away. Not sure about giving the booze up either, ain't much point is there? Course I ain't murdered anyone, it was stupid of me to think that I'd do something like that. Feel bad for the old fella though, poor geezer only come round for a drink and now he's brown bread, can't believe that snide bastard would kill someone. I wonder why he did it? I'm gonna go down the pub and see what's happening, thank God the vodka made me see clearly.

Fuck it, I'm going to have to go down the pub and see if anyone knows anything, I can't just phone up the old bill, I don't know what the score is. I need some advice and I can't ask the missus, she'll just drag me down the police station. Out the door and I fly down the stairs, I just want this to be all over, there don't seem to be that many police about anymore though. In the door of the pub and there's no one in there apart from that geezer that watches the races all day. There's a pint on the bar but no one sitting there. The girl behind the bar takes no notice of me.

"Give us a pint please, love."

"You heard about that poor old man? Terrible ain't it?"

"Yeah, who was he?"

"What? You don't know?"

The door to the toilet opens and the old boy walks out, sits down at the bar and drinks half a pint in one go. I look at him like I've seen a ghost. He turns and looks at me.

"Some fucking night we had last night, I don't remember getting home. Never drinking with your maniac friend again. In fact, I don't think I'll ever speak to you two wankers ever again."

His jacket has got red all over it.

"What happened to your jacket?"

"Your mate went completely mental after you left, went into his room came out with a pot of red ink and started throwing it around the room. Look at my jacket! You need to have words with him, sort him out."

"Yeah..."

Well this is a bit unexpected, Rob and the old boy are standing at the bar, the old boy's got red stuff all over his jacket and Rob's just standing there staring at him. They've been in here all day and I've been wandering about worrying. How comes there was old bill all over the place this morning? What's all that red stuff all over the wall? I need a drink.

"Vodka and Coke please, Claire."

"You've got a cheek ain't ya? Look at his jacket. You need to be getting him a new one."

"Yeah, sorry mate. I'll be honest, I don't remember what happened."

"You threw a load of red ink all over him last night, went mental apparently. Where the fuck did you get red ink from?"

"I ain't really sure, it's one of them things that I found in my room after a night on the piss, I might have nicked it. Why is there coppers everywhere?"

"Some kids robbed an old man last night, he fell and ended up dead. Fucking terrible."

"Rob, lend us £20, mate, I'm a bit short at the moment, I'll sort you out in a few weeks. How come you ain't at work?"

"Called in sick, couldn't be arsed with it today. Where you been, I was looking for you?"

"Just went for a walk. Get us a double vodka and coke, mate!"

Chinese Whispers

I was speaking to June down the way the other night. You know that woman that lives over at number 57? The one with short brown hair and a couple of kids? You see her sometimes waiting for them outside the school, really quiet, doesn't seem to have much to do with anyone? Yeah, her, well anyway, June was telling me that she saw her buying a bottle of vodka in the supermarket the other day, you wouldn't think much of it but I saw her the day before and she was buying one then as well. A bottle of vodka a day and she's looking after a couple of kids?

Her old man left her a few years back, apparently he just packed his bags and left one day. I reckon it was because she was drinking all the time, what sort of man would be able to put up with that. She's got this new boyfriend that comes round and sees her. Looks like a nice geezer, well dressed, don't think he's from around here, never seen him before. I wonder how long she'll last with him, I doubt he'll be putting up with that kind of carry on for long. It's them kids that I feel sorry for the most though, imagine coming home to find your mother pissed every night? Shocking!

What a terrible couple of days it's been! I've a few friends coming round on Saturday evening so I've been tidying the flat up and trying to buy a few things in. I went and bought a large bottle of vodka yesterday morning and then knocked it off the worktop when I was cleaning. I had to go and get a new one this morning, money's a bit tight at the moment, so it really hasn't helped but I can't have them round and not have any drink for them. I've not seen them in years, I'm really looking forward to it, let my hair down just for the one night.

The kids have been a bit of a nightmare too which don't help when you're trying to organise things. James was messing about on his bed and fell off it now he's got a massive bruise on his leg, I hope no one sees it, people will think I'm a terrible mother. I shouldn't complain really, he's a good kid, loves doing his school work. I'm just a bit worried that he's so quiet, he don't really have many friends either and I don't know what to do about it, I don't want to put any pressure on him but I'm worried the other kids will bully him.

It'd have been so much easier if their father had've stayed around but I couldn't put up with that anymore. I was sick and tired of hearing what a nice person he was, how well he treated me and how grateful I should be. He was a sneaky bastard, only got abusive when the doors were closed and nobody could see. That night I took the knife from the kitchen and told him I'd kill him if he didn't leave was the best thing I ever did. I'm just worried that it's had a bad effect on James, might be why he's so quiet.

The little one has just started school but she's completely different. She just don't stop talking to people, she hasn't got that from me I can tell you that. One of her teachers reckons she's got a lot of potential, I'm so proud of her. She don't seem to have been affected by her father, she don't even ask about him. I'm thinking about signing her up for some dance classes, she loves dancing. I'll give up smoking, that same money would be better spent on her. It's one of my few pleasures but I'd rather see her doing something that makes her happy.

Since he's been gone it's been hard, money's been tight. I do the odd little cleaning job here and there, gives us a few extra quid. I hardly ever have time to go out myself, not that I have too many friends. He was so controlling. Now that I'm free I find it really hard to make friends, I don't have the time, I just find it hard to talk to people. That's why I'm so excited that my friends are coming round. We used to go to school together and I haven't seen them for years.

It's awful ain't it? All these immigrants moving in around here, we won't know ourselves in a few years' time. I met that little Johnny kid's mum the other day when I was out shopping, she was telling me about that woman that lives at number 57. Reckons she's drinking a couple of bottles of vodka a day, seen her in the supermarket stocking up. Funny thing is, I was walking past the house that drug dealer lives in a couple of weeks back, I could have sworn I seen her coming out of there, I ain't sure but it looked like her.

My John is in the same class as one of the kids at school, he says the kid don't say nothing when they are in class, quiet as a mouse. When they was getting dressed for P.E he said the kid had a big bruise on his leg. I don't like to gossip, you know me, I don't talk about anyone but that ain't right, especially if she's knocking back a couple of bottles of vodka a day, if she's on drugs as well God knows what she's doing to them poor children. I've half a mind to phone up the social but well you can't be sure can ya?

James came home from school today and said one of the other kids told him he wasn't allowed to play with him, his mum had told him that I was a bad lady and that he was to stay away from James. Who do these people think they are? None of them even know me. I do my little jobs, I take the kids to school, I pick them up, I try to do everything I can for them. What makes them think that I'm a bad person. I wouldn't care what they think or are saying about me if it wasn't for James, he's so quiet anyway, how is he ever going to make any friends?

One of my jobs told me today that they won't need me anymore as they have too many people there and I was the last one that joined. I'm going to have to find something else quickly, it's James' birthday soon and I want to try and have a little party for him. I was going to ask some of the other kids' mums but if they are talking like that I don't know if I should now. I don't want him just to have it on his own with his sister though. I suppose it might just be the one person, maybe the other mums don't think the same.

The little party I had the other night was great, really nice to be able to let my hair down for a night. Jenny was dancing in the living room with my two friends, James even got up for a while and danced with them. It was so nice to see him being a little bit more outgoing. It's funny, after going and buying that new bottle of vodka we didn't drink anything at all, they don't drink anymore and I hardly ever drink at all so I didn't bother. They were saying I should try and move out to where they live but how would I find the money to do that?

I have been really lonely recently, it's a real struggle but I try and keep a brave face on for the kids. I see a lot of the other mums round here going out on a Friday night and I wish I was able to do that too. Thing is, I feel guilty about wanting to go out and enjoy myself, I don't want to leave the kids with a stranger, it's stupid I know but I feel a little bit like I'd be neglecting them by going out for the night. The other problem is, who would I go out with? I can't just walk into the pub on my own.

My brother, Dan, he's good to me and the kids. I might ask him if he'll look after them for me, just for the one night. He's been coming round a lot recently to make sure me and the kids are okay. He's one of the only people that can have long conversations with James too. He didn't come for years when I was with 'him'. I hated Dan for it, but we've made up since and now he seems to want to make amends. I'm not sure that Dan really believed that he was as bad as he was. No one did. At least we've got a good relationship now.

Did you hear the noise coming out her flat the other night? They was having a right party in there, went on until well late. I was about to go round there but the music stopped. I had a look out the window when her friends were leaving and she was swaying all over the place, she was in a right state. The two kids were still up as well, not that they'd be able to sleep with all that noise. I wonder how many bottles of vodka she got through?! I told Jack he ain't to play with the boy, I don't want no bad influences on him, I feel sorry for the boy but I ain't getting my Jack involved with them people.

I was talking to the woman that lives above them the other day, I seen her outside the school, she reckons she used to knock her husband about. She used to hear shouting and screaming, he was such a quiet man, there's no way I could see him touching her, it must have been her going mad after

*she'd been drinking all day. Poor fella, I bet he doesn't go and
see the kids because she won't let him see them. That boy is
so quiet, I bet he really misses his dad, I think someone should
do something about it really, it ain't fair on them poor kids.*

James came home with a letter from his teacher today, she
said that the homework he'd done was brilliant. I've never
been so proud! We spent hours together doing that
homework, it was writing a story about a place far away. I
never realised he had such an imagination. I felt as nervous
as him when he went through the gates at school, I can't
wipe the smile of my face. He keeps taking the story out of
his bag and reading it again and again. I'm starting to think he
might be getting over his father. I asked my brother if he'd
lend me a few quid for the birthday party, he said it was no
problem.

Jenny's signed up for the dance classes, she starts next week.
I'm a bit unsure about whether I want her to go now though,
she said one of the other girls in her class was nasty to her,
said her mum was poor and didn't buy her any new clothes,
the other little girl said I was a bad lady too, like the boy said
to James. I really don't understand where all this is coming

from. If it keeps going on I'm going to have say something, I don't want these poisonous people making my children's lives a misery. I'm starting to think I need to find a way of getting out of here. A new start.

They all talk about other people and don't look at themselves. The other day when I was in the supermarket buying that bottle of vodka I saw one of the other mums in there, she looked at me like I was dirt, stupid thing was, I never buy booze but there she was putting a couple of crates of beer into her trolley. I wonder if that's the mum of that kid that said something to James? I bet it is you know. Stupid cow! Fuck her anyway, I hate swearing even if it is to myself but she's made me so angry! She better not be going around saying it to other people.

I asked my brother about looking after the kids for a night and he said it was no problem, so next Friday, for the first time in years I'm going out on my own for the night! I'm a bit nervous about it if I'm honest, especially if there are people talking about me. I wonder if Lucy is free? She said I could go out and stay with her for a night if I wanted to. It'd be better than going into that pub on my own, I'm sure he won't mind looking after them for an extra few hours. He enjoys being with the kids and they like being with him too. Just so I can get away for a day.

I'll have to ask a few of the mothers at school if their kids will come to James's party tomorrow. I was going to knock on the neighbour's door but it's probably better to ask them at the school. I'm going shopping tomorrow when I've done my morning job, I can't wait, I'm really excited about the party for him, I want to make it the best I can. Dan gave me a few quid extra to get Jenny a new dress that she can wear at the party too, I've told her she can ask two of her friends from her class if they want to come.

You ain't going to believe this! That alcoholic woman with the two kids, well I was talking to her next door neighbour the other day and apparently she left the kids all night with that new fella of hers while she swanned off out on the piss somewhere. Imagine leaving your kids with someone you've only known for five minutes!? I think it's disgusting, she thinks she's all high and mighty as well, never see her talk to any of the mums when she comes to pick the kids up, I reckon she thinks she's better than all of us.

Sharon told me she seen her coming out of a drug dealers house a few weeks back, I didn't believe that but she said na, it was definitely her. The little girl is joining the dance class next week, it's a wonder that she finds the money for it, what with her drinking all day and probably smoking crack. I know she does a few cleaning jobs, don't know how if she's out of her nut all the time, wouldn't be surprised if she's doing it so she can nick stuff from the places she's working in. I seen her with a dress the other day but no bag.

James came home crying yesterday, he wouldn't tell me what was wrong with him but I'm guessing it's the other kids saying things to him. He seemed to have moved on so much, I don't want him to start going backwards again. Jenny has been a bit quiet lately too, she said she didn't want to go to her first dance class but she's promised that she'll go next week. I have to find a way of sorting all this out, I need to know who's spreading all these rumours, there has to be someone. These kids must be hearing it from their mothers.

I asked some of the mums if the kids wanted to come to the party but they all said the kids had something to do. I went and had a word with James's teacher and she said he was very quiet but she didn't think any of the other kids were picking on him. When I told him that it'll just be me his sister and my brother at his birthday party he was delighted. I suppose if that makes him happier it's better but I really do want him to have some friends, even one. I've been thinking of ways to get out of here, I like our little flat but this can't go on.

It was great going to Lucy's last Friday, I was worrying about the kids a lot but I still managed to relax. Dan said he had a great time with the kids. It'd be good if I could try and do it once a month, just so I can have a little bit of time to myself. Still have that little bit of a guilty feeling though. I know I shouldn't but I can't help it, I'm trying to give them the best I can and things have been so difficult for them recently. I think I know which of the mothers is going around and spreading these rumours. I'm plucking up the courage to go and knock on her door.

She was giving me dirty looks outside the school the other day. Don't know what she's looking at me like that for. I've only been telling people the truth, people deserve to know who their kids are playing with. At least I can hold my head up high and know that I ain't like that. I think they should take the kids out of the school, maybe take them off her, I know it ain't their fault but the apple don't fall far from the tree and all that. She better not say anything to me.

You know what I'll do? I'll write her a letter and put it through the letterbox and tell her all about herself. She needs to know what she's doing ain't right, not looking after them kids, leaving them with that stranger while she goes off to get pissed all the time. You know what makes me angry? She looks at us all like we're pieces of dirt when she's at the school, she ain't any better than any of us, I hope they take the kids off her, that would serve her right, the father should have taken them with him really but I suppose he couldn't if she ain't right in the head.

A letter come through the door yesterday morning. It was anonymous but the stuff written inside it was awful. Saying I was a terrible mother and how I shouldn't be buying booze early in the mornings, that letting my kids stay with a strange man while I go out on the piss means I'm neglecting my kids. Why would anyone do this? Are their lives that unimportant that they have to make things up about me and then put letters through my door threatening to have my kids taken off me? Am I really doing the best for them or am I lying to myself?

I feel like I'm starting to crack up. The way that people are looking at me around here, I know I shouldn't take any notice but it's hard not to, especially when it's affecting the kids. Jenny is starting to go inside herself, she don't talk as much as she used to and she don't want to go to these dance classes. She said the other kids at school are talking about her. James came home with a cut on the side of his face the other day. When I asked him what had happened he wouldn't tell me. I'm going to have to go and see the teacher.

I thought I was really strong, after what happened with their dad and all that, I thought I could cope with anything but I'm starting to feel like I'm not a good mum anymore. I can barely afford to give them the things that they want, I've lost another two cleaning jobs and I didn't get a reason why. My brother says everything will work out okay but I can't see any light at the end of the tunnel at the moment. There really is no escape. I want to say something to that bitch of a woman, but if I'm honest I'm scared, everywhere I've gone the last week or so people have been giving me dirty looks.

I've asked Dan to look after the kids tonight, take them over to his so I can have a night to myself here at home. I need some time to think about how I'm going to get away, I can't keep the kids in an environment like this. To be honest I want a night to myself so I can just sit down and cry my eyes out and no one will know. I can't let the kids see me being weak. We've got this far, we'll find a way. I've bought myself a bottle of wine, I know I shouldn't really, I can't afford it but I just need a night to relax.

Maybe after I've drank the wine I'll have the courage to go round and tell that fucking woman what I think of her and tell her to stop interfering in our lives. Jesus, how can one person have such an effect on my life? Someone I don't even fucking know. I must be a lot stronger than I thought, it'd have driven most people mad by now. Or am I going mad? I am treating the kids properly aren't I? We don't have much but I do the best for them. Fuck it, I can't keep going on like this, I'm going round her house to sort this all out, I'll just go upstairs and change my clothes.

I told you didn't I? Told you she was always pissed, she was definitely on drugs as well, you don't end up like that if you ain't on something. Lucky her kids weren't there, it would have been terrible for them to see something like that. Probably the only good thing she's ever done sending them round that fellas house that night, someone said he's her brother but I don't believe that, he don't even look like her, people are just trying to make excuses now, they always do that don't they? When they feel sorry for someone?

I wonder what they'll do with the kids? Probably put them into care or something. I always said I felt sorry for them and I was right. I was speaking to the girl that lives next door to her, she said the fella found her at the bottom of the stairs in the morning. She'd fallen down them and broken her neck. Definitely had to be pissed. If it was anyone else I'd say it was a terrible way to go, but not her, it'll be better for the kids. I'll tell you something else, that girl that lives next door to her, I ain't sure about her at all, when I was speaking to her I was sure there was something not quite right

Saturday

It's my favourite day of the week. Saturday morning, sitting on the balcony watching the path leading up to our block, waiting to catch a sight of him, tall with black hair. Then waiting for the buzzer to ring so that I can let him in. I look at the clock through the doorway, it's almost 10. He'll be here any minute. If he's a few minutes late I start to worry and panic, thinking that he might not turn up, that something has happened to him, that I will never see him again. Butterflies in my stomach as I see him walk up the path, he looks up and waves, I rush to the intercom to open the door.

Every other day I watch the other kids meeting their dads at the school gates, see their smiles and happiness as they walk home together. I see them out on the green playing football with their dads in the evenings, going out to buy things from the shop together. It doesn't make me sad, well maybe a little bit, I know that on Saturday I'll be able to do the same. I wish it was more than just Saturday though, I wish it was every day. What can I do though? I am just a kid, I don't know why adults do what they do.

All Friday afternoon I sit in the classroom excited, that's when the butterflies start. I think about what I am going to tell him when he arrives on Saturday morning. Should I tell him about my week, what I did at school or what I did with my friends? I want to tell him that I've been chosen for the school football team, I want him to be proud of me. The boy that sits next to me doesn't have a dad at all, he never sees him. I feel sorry for him, at least I see my dad once a week. That boy doesn't even know what his dad looks like.

I remember the day that he left. He told me that he was going away for a few weeks, my mum was crying. He had a big bag that he'd put all his clothes in. He hugged me and then kissed my forehead and then walked out the door. I watched as he walked down the path and over the green. I thought I would never see him again, I didn't cry though, but I wanted to. I didn't want mum to see me crying, I wanted to try and make her smile. I hugged her and she held me tightly, she told me not to worry, everything would be okay, I don't think she really thought that though.

He comes in the door, picks me up and spins me around, I laugh. He's so tall, I hope I will be as tall as him when I am older. I sit in the living room watching television while he talks to mum, they don't argue anymore. I wonder if he will come back one day? I wish he would, he could wait outside the gates for me when I finish school, we could talk every day, we could watch football on the telly together. Mum says he will never come back for good but I think he will one day, I really do think that they love each other.

He calls me from the kitchen and we get ready to go out. Mum tells me to make sure that I keep warm and to ring her later to let her know what time I will be home. Dad tells her not to worry, he's going to take me to Nanny's and then we'll go and play football, if we're going to be late he'll let her know. I'm so excited that I can't say anything, I want to say something but the words just won't come out. Mum ruffles my hair and says goodbye, we walk down the stairs instead of taking the lift, he doesn't like the lift.

Halfway down the stairs we meet someone he knows.

"You taking him out for the day?"

"Yeah, gonna take him down me mom's for a bit and then go to the park and play football. He's a good little footballer, you know?"

His friend looks at me and laughs, I want to explode with pride.

"He's a bit quiet ain't he?"

"Just the way he is, where you off to?"

"Down the betting shop and then down the pub. You around later?"

"I'll see, depends what time we get back. I'll catch you later."

"Later mate."

Why do people always say I am quiet? When they say I am quiet it makes me scared to talk. I feel my face go red, dad doesn't seem to care though, he always just says 'that's the way he is'.

"Why do people say I'm quiet?"

"Haha, don't worry about them mate, they don't know you, some people talk too much, if other people don't talk as much as them they think they're quiet. Even if you are quiet, what does it matter? We talk a lot don't we?"

"Yeah..."

We wait at the underground station for the train to come. Every time we are here I hope that I'll see a red tube train, I've never seen one, each week dad says we'll see one next week. As we stand on the platform and the wind starts to come out of the tunnel I hope that it's going to be a red one, not one of them boring, dirty grey ones. My friend said he saw one last week but I don't believe him, I think he was lying. The tracks start to rattle, the lights from the front of the train appear in the tunnel, it bursts into the station and it's red, the first time I've ever seen one.

"I told you we'd see one this week!"

We sit on the train, dad tells me if a ticket inspector gets on the train we have to run. As the train pulls into each station I look at every person to see if they are an inspector. None in this station. There was one last week so we jumped off the train and ran up the stairs and walked the rest of the way. Dad always tells me not to tell mum, I never do, I don't think she'd care though. We reach our stop and climb up the stairs, it seems so far away from home even though it isn't.

"We'll go to the shop first, do you want some sweets?"

"Okay..."

The shop is old but it has everything, I don't know what most of the things are for. The shelves at the top have old typewriters and model planes on them. On the shelf below are footballs and other sport things. At the back of the shop are rows and rows of little plastic tubs that are filled with sweets. Coca cola bottles, shrimps, flying saucers and lollipops. I take my time choosing which ones I want, mum doesn't let me buy them, she says they're bad for my teeth so I won't be able to get anymore until next time dad brings me here.

I choose 10 cola bottles and 10 white golf balls that taste like mint. Dad pays for them and when we get outside he pulls a magazine from under his coat and gives it to me. It's a football magazine full of pictures. He laughs as he gives it to me.

"Tell your mum I bought it."

We walk through the market to nanny's house, when we walk in the door I can smell food. Bacon, eggs, sausages, black pudding. She puts the plates down in front of both of us.

"I hope there's enough there now"

"Course it's enough mom."

Dad reads the Racing Post as he eats his food. Saturday mornings will always be the smell of the sweet shop and the smell of fried food at nanny's house.

"Isn't that poor child cold?"

"Nah, he's alright, ain't ya mate?"

"Yeah, I'm okay"

"Jesus, he's nothing on him."

"Leave him alone, there's nothing wrong with him."

"Where you taking him today?"

"Just go down the park for a bit. Might go in the pub for a bit later if you want to come over?"

"Jesus, why would I be going to the pub? What time will you be there?"

"I don't know, we'll see, I'll give you a bell when we get there."

"If there's no answer, I'm shopping. Make sure you look after that child, you don't want him catching a cold. Do you have any tips for today?"

"I haven't had a look at the paper properly yet, you keep talking to me."

"Put a bet on for me later. Do you know Mrs O'Malley?"

"That old girl that goes in the pub?"

"Jesus, I saw her yesterday and wasn't she crawling down the road. Fuckin' polluted she was, and no fucker would help her up."

"Shocking ain't it?"

"Ah sure, what can you do?"

"Come on mate, we'll go down the park for a bit. Say goodbye to Nanny."

"Bye…"

"Don't tell your father," she says as she puts £20 in my hand, "and don't catch a cold, Mrs Dwyer's son caught a cold the other week and now he's in hospital with pneumonia. The poor fucker will be lucky to see the week out."

We walk back through the market, dad saying hello to the people who work on the stalls. I don't usually like places with lots of people but I love it here on a Saturday morning. People buying their fruit and veg for their dinners, the stall owners hanging around talking about football, old men waiting outside the pubs for the doors to open. Dad knows everyone, I feel safe, I wish I didn't have to leave him at the end of the day, I want it to go on forever.

"How did that man get sick?"

"Which man?"

"The one nanny said was in hospital because he had a cold"

"Ohhh, haha, he didn't have a cold, he fell asleep outside on his way home from the pub so he got pneumonia. Mrs Dwyer is telling everyone he had a cold."

"Is nanny going to come to the pub?"

"I don't know mate, probably. Don't lose that 20 quid she gave you, give it to your mum when you get home."

"Dad..."

"Yes, mate?

"Do you think I can be a footballer when I grow up?"

"Of course you can mate, you need to work hard though, practice a lot. You go out and play with your mates don't you?"

"Yeah, every day."

"You'll be alright, I'll be there when you score the winning goal at Wembley."

Walking to the park is my favourite part of the day, especially in the autumn. The leaves are falling on the floor, I run through the piles and throw them in the air. There are conkers all over the pavement, I pick them up and put them in my pocket, dad looks at them to see which ones are the best.

"When you get home make sure you put them in vinegar."

The sky is blue, really light blue, it's cold but I don't really feel it. In the distance there are two tower blocks that have been closed down, no one lives in them. I don't know why but I love looking at them, two white empty towers with their square windows and nobody living in them. They look like something out of one of them TV shows you see on Sunday morning, one of them programmes about the future. They make my imagination go crazy, I would love to spend a day inside one of them, all on my own, exploring.

"Why does no one live in them two tower blocks?"

"Asbestos, it's bad for you so nobody is allowed to live in them anymore."

"Oh, what's asbestos?"

"They put it in people's homes to keep the flat warm."

"Oh, what will they do with them?"

"Knock them down probably. I remember when they were building them, your nanny was offered one of them flats, lucky she didn't take it."

The park is empty, not many people wanting to come down here on a cold morning. The ground is muddy and hard, I run around kicking the ball as dad pretends to be a football commentator. I laugh as he falls over trying to kick the ball. He rolls on the ground and moans, I run over to him, worried he's hurt himself badly, when I reach him he turns over and starts laughing and pulls me down to the floor as well. He jumps up runs over to the ball and runs away with it. I can't chase him because I'm still laughing.

I sit on the swings while dad reads the Racing Post in peace. I try to imagine what mum is doing now. I wonder if she misses dad? I used to hate it when they argued all the time, at least now they don't argue at all. If he came back would they start arguing again? Sometimes I used to think it was my fault but I know it wasn't, every week dad tells me it wasn't my fault that he left. Every week nanny tells him he's an idiot for leaving us. I think she thinks I don't understand but I do, maybe if he won lots of money on the horses he'll come back again.

"Come on mate, time to go, we'll go up the pub for a couple of hours and then I'll take you back to your mother's."

"Can I stay tonight?"

"Not tonight mate, your nan doesn't have much space. Maybe next week."

The pub smells of old beer and cigarettes. Nanny is already there, she has a cigarette in one hand and a half pint in the other. She's talking to one of her friends. I can't remember what her name is, they all look the same, stiff curly hair, glasses, and an accent that I don't really understand when they're drunk. One of the old men stands up and starts singing, some of the other people tell him to shut up and sit down. Dad buys himself a pint and buys me a coke. Nanny tells him to buy her another drink.

"Did you put a bet on for me?"

"Nah, I'll nip over to the bookies now, I can't take him in there with me. Stay here with your nan for a minute, mate, I'll be back soon."

Nanny goes back to talking to her friend. There's an old man at the bar drinking Guinness, he doesn't talk to anyone, just sitting there drinking and smoking. There's horse racing on the television, a group of men sitting underneath it, one of them scrunches up a white paper slip and throws it on the floor and walks over to the bar to order a drink. Every time someone comes in through the door I check to see if it's dad. Nanny goes to the bar to buy another drink, the woman she is talking to just sits there looking at me not saying anything.

A man comes out of the toilet rubbing his nose, his face is red and his eyes are moving everywhere. He taps his friend on the back and they laugh loudly, they're shouting at each other but they're joking. The man who came out of the toilet pulls out a big load of money from his pocket and gives it to his friend, he pats him on the back again and walks out of the pub. A glass breaks on the floor and there are loud cheers and then laughter, the bar maid looks angry. I see one of dad's friends standing at the bar and he winks at me, he shouts over, "He'll be back in a minute." I relax a little bit.

Dad comes back into the pub and sits down next to me.

"You okay mate? Sorry, took a bit longer than I thought. Do you want another coke?"

"No, I'm okay."

"Okay, I'll just go and get another drink, I'll get you a packet of crisps."

We sit there together in silence, dad drinking his pint, me eating my crisps and drinking my coke. He salutes people as they come through the door. I feel better with him sitting next to me, I was a bit scared when just nanny was there, all the people in here know me, but I was scared they would talk to me because I wouldn't know what to say back to them. Dad buys another drink for him and nanny. Nanny starts singing songs in her mixed Dublin/London accent. Dad looks at me and laughs, there are a bunch of wires at the back of the chair, he pretends to pull them.

"We'll all go together..."

"Will you fuck off and stop frightening the poor child."

"He ain't scared are ya mate?"

I just laugh, I'm not scared, I think it's funny. Nanny says she's going home, she's had enough for tonight. Dad looks at his watch and says he had better take me back to my mother. It's dark outside.

"We'll walk home shall we?"

"Okay!"

"I'll take you away somewhere next year mate, we'll go on holiday, just me and you. I'm a bit skint at the moment. We'll go to Spain or somewhere like that."

"I remember when we went to Portugal, you, me and mum, you fell asleep and got sunburnt."

"Yeah, we watched the 1986 World Cup final in Portuguese. They were good times them. Your mum's a good woman you know, mate? She looks after you."

"I know she is."

We walk in silence, he seems lost in his own thoughts. I don't usually see him like that. I don't want to ask him what the matter is though. I wish when we get home that he wouldn't leave, he'd just stay but I know he's not going to. That's why I wanted to walk home, just to spend an extra hour with him. We walk down the backstreets, the tall buildings of our estates coming into view, most of the lights are on. I bet all my friends are sitting in with their dads watching television or having dinner with them.

"Dad..."

"Yes mate?"

"Will you ever come home?"

"No mate, I'm not going to come back home."

I look down at the floor, I want to ask another question but I can't, if I start speaking I'll start crying as well. I can feel the back of my throat tighten, tears in my eyes. He sounded sad when he said it.

"Everything will be okay mate. I love your mum but we just can't live together. We argue too much and it ain't fair on you. You don't want all that again. You make sure you look after your mum though, she needs you."

"I will..."

"I need to tell you something mate, I've got a new girlfriend. I don't live at nanny's anymore. I didn't want to tell you because I thought it would upset you. She said you can stay on Saturday nights if you want. You'll like her, she's nice."

"Oh..."

"She's going to be having a baby too, you'll be having a little brother or sister."

"I won't be an only child anymore."

"Haha, no mate you won't."

"Does mum know?"

"Yeah, she knows."

"Oh..."

"Don't get upset, mate. I'll love you all the same, just when she has the baby I might not be able to come around every Saturday morning. I'll make it up to you though."

"Will we still be able to go on holiday together?"

"Of course we will. I promise."

I always thought that they would get back together. I just thought they wanted a rest from each other and then one day he'd come back with his bag and put all his stuff back in the wardrobe. Now that's never going to happen. What if he loves the new baby more than he loves me? What if he doesn't come around on Saturdays ever again? I won't have anything to look forward to during the week anymore. I can't fight back the tears, I cry. He puts his hand on my shoulder and stops me.

"Whatever happens mate, I'll always love you, your mum will always love you. I know you wanted us to get back together but it won't happen. I promise I will never let you down again."

We reach the bottom of our block. Dad opens the door and I run up the stairs, I don't hug him like I usually do. He waits until I am inside the house, I don't wave at him like I usually do either, I just look out the window. He walks off with is head down. I look over at the two empty tower blocks, I wish more than ever that I could run off to them, go there where nobody can find me and cry. Mum comes into my room and hugs me, she knows.

"I'm sorry, love."

Just Another Day

Jesus, I'm so tired. Only a few hours' sleep and I have to get up. Palm trees, turquoise sea, golden sand, that's what I need, I'd take it just for an hour. To get away, relax, not have to worry, a servant would have to be thrown in as well; someone could do something for me for a few hours. Can dream hey? The sun is shining outside, the sky is blue, no beach though, definitely no servant, just grey, dreary looking blocks of flats. Why did they ever make them like this? If they'd have made them nice looking I bet it would have made a difference. Didn't have to live in them though did they?

Really didn't make much last night, I've got to do a bit of shopping as well, I'm trying to look after myself a bit more, eat healthily, it ain't cheap though. There's some fella upstairs, very well spoken, his mate has opened a vegetable plot on the top floor, on the roof. I wonder how much their vegetables are? Not cheap I expect, don't understand what they're doing around here, it's fucking mad, they look like completely out of place. There's a rumour they're selling gear out of the juice bar they opened. Only way they'd get any business.

I took the mirror off the wall the other week, I don't want to see myself as I get up in the morning. I'm tired at looking at those tired eyes. I suppose I don't look too bad for 45, one of the fellas at work said I look 30 the other day. Nice to hear things like that even if I know he's only trying to be nice. I'll put it back up in a few weeks time and see if eating these vegetables and drinking those horrible shakes has made any difference. Probably easier to just put a couple of cucumbers over my eyes, cheaper as well.

What shall I wear? I'm only going to the shop, these leggings will do, I'll throw that pink t-shirt on as well, it doesn't look like it's too cold out there. That's another thing I wish I could do, buy some new clothes, oh well, I'll get my break someday I'm sure. Go on, I'll have a quick look in the mirror. Not too bad I suppose, maybe that fella was right, not sure about 30 though, 35 will do! Right! Let's face the world.

You'll never amount to nothing! You're fucking useless! Do you not know why all those other kids pick on you? It's because you're thick. Look at you, you've got no friends, you spend all your time moping about the house, what do you do to help me? Nothing, you're selfish, you don't realise what I have to do to keep you fed and make sure you've got clothes. As soon as you're old enough you're out that door to fend for yourself, I don't care what you're mother thinks. You turned 10 last week and you still act like a baby. Why can't you be like your sister?

This woman that's at the checkout lives on the same floor as me. She's one of them that thinks she can't do anything wrong, thinks she's perfect. Whenever I see her she looks down her nose at me. Don't know what makes her think she's so different from everyone else. Funny, I saw her the other week walking her dog, one of them horrible, aggressive little things, the dog bit some man that was walking down the street. He went mad, said the dog should be put down and he was going to call the R.S.P.C.A, she weren't looking down her nose at him then. I want to say I hope he did but it'd be the animal that gets hurt. I don't like it but I wouldn't want it hurt.

I've bought a load of vegetables, some of them I don't really know what they are, I must look like a right weirdo. The man in front of me has got a shopping trolley full of sausages, nothing else just sausages. I bet his kids can't wait for dinner! 'What's for dinner dad?'. 'Sausages'. She smiles at him, you can look down your nose at your neighbour but you can't at a man with a shopping trolley full of sausages. Maybe he's having a barbecue, I hope his guests like sausages. How's he going to get all of them home? Probably got a car.

He walks off with his trolley. She has that look on her face. I smile, I know it's fake but at least I'm trying. She runs the stuff through the checkout, doesn't say a word when the bill comes up on the till, I hand her the money, she gives back my change, dropping it in my hand like she doesn't want to touch me in any way. I smile at her one last time, I can see she hates it, she hates that her dislike of me has no effect, that I don't care. I do care, of course I care, you always care when someone treats you like you're shit, but I'm never going to show her that.

Walking along the high street, it's empty for this time of the morning. Usually there's more people out shopping, everyone must be skint. I notice the geezer with the sausages on the other side of the road. He's pushing a trolley with all of the sausages still inside. Is that how our estate ends up with a load of shopping trolleys lying around? It's this geezer carting his sausages back from the supermarket. I wonder if the ones in the canal are because of him too? I don't know why I'm even thinking about this. It's amazing the nonsense you think up while you're walking about.

It's your birthday tomorrow, don't think I've forgotten, you better make sure all your stuff is packed, you're out that door. You can have breakfast, I'll let you have that, think of it as a birthday present. After that you're on your own. All these years I've looked after you, given you everything, and you still ain't making nothing of yourself. I'd wish you luck but there ain't really no hope that you'll make something of yourself is there? Look at your sister out there working every day while you're sat around here feeling sorry for yourself.

There's loads of kids in the little playground at the bottom of the block. It must be the school holidays. Yeah, it's May, they have a week off. I'll sit down for a bit before I go back upstairs, be good to get some fresh air. The kids are running around after each other, laughing and arguing about whatever game they're playing. One of the little girls starts crying and walks away to sit on the bench next to me. She stops crying when she sits down. She takes no notice of me even though I'm looking at her, she looks like Claire, it's not her but I can't stop looking at her.

I'm back 20 years ago in the same place, sitting on the same bench. It's still the same, same blocks of flats, same people, they're just twenty years younger. She's there playing on the swing, going back and forth, waving at me. I'm so proud of her! She stops the swing and runs over to me, giving me a hug and then running back to the climbing frame and sliding down the slide over and over. I call out to her, tell her it's time to go home. She skips over, taking my hand and we walk off to the entrance to the block and up the stairs where I'll read her a story before she goes to bed.

The little girl has gone, I didn't notice. She's back playing with the other kids, happy again. She'll be 25 now. I wonder what she's doing with her life? She was clever, she probably went to university and got herself a good job, nothing like me. I sit here each day and hope that she might turn up to find me. It was our favourite place. She wouldn't even know what I look like, I'd know it was her though. Why did I mess it all up so badly? I believed what he told me, I believed I was worthless, I suppose I still do.

Back upstairs, I hear a kid scream. I'm back there again, the day they came and took her off me, she was only six, in one year it had all gone so wrong. Screaming as they took her down the stairs, me shouting back, telling her that it was all going to be okay, she'd only be gone for a little while, I've not seen her since. I wish there was another way to get up to the flat, but there ain't, I have to walk this three or four times a day. I hear it every single time, that scream, I don't know if it's in my head or if someone really is screaming.

You're not fit to raise a child. It's that simple. Your lifestyle is not one that will produce a good environment for a child to grow up in. I'm sure that you know that yourself. If, and it's a big if, you can sort your life out, there is a chance you'll get her back. You need to make an effort though, you have to stop taking heroin and find a means of making money that is not illegal. Do these things and circumstances might change. It's up to you, it's your choice, I know you didn't have an easy childhood yourself and so I expect you understand why this has happened.

I need to tidy the flat up. It's tidy but it gives me something to do. It's the same each day, I wake up feeling okay, positive and as the day goes on it gets darker and darker, stuck in the same cycle and I don't know how to get out of it. When I'm tidying up I don't have to think so much, it takes my mind away from that cycle. I wonder what that man with the sausages is doing? Probably still pushing his trolley around. That woman at the checkout I wonder who she's sneering at now? Some unfortunate person that has never done a bad thing in their life.

If I ran away, what could I do? This coffee table is a mess, I need to get a new one. Where could I go? I should throw it out really but I can't afford a new one. Can't afford a coffee table and I'm thinking about running away. Not going to get very far am I? I'd love to just get on a train one day and get off at the last stop and start a new life. It wouldn't work though would it? It isn't the place that matters, it'll all keep following me around. Those windows are filthy, I'll have to do that before I go out this evening.

I could go back to school. I forgot to buy cleaning stuff, I can't be bothered to go out again, soapy water will have to do. Go back to school and do what though? It ain't changing anything, I could go back to school, become the best solicitor in the world and it still wouldn't change anything, it'd still be running. I might just throw that coffee table out, I can do without one, it'd be something less to clean though and that wouldn't be good. How do I change all this though? I don't know, that's the problem.

The geezer with the sausages, did he even notice me? What did he think when he saw me? A woman with a load of vegetables in her basket, probably thought pretentious bitch. Or he could have just thought nothing, she's just a woman doing her shopping. You can't tell can you? I make all these judgements about him and yet I don't know anything about him. Why does cleaning make me get all philosophical? Jean, will be home soon, I'll go round and have a cup of coffee at hers, at least it's someone to talk to.

You've sorted yourself though, I know you're not living a perfect life, but if she did come and find you, she'd know you weren't the person you were. You know what? You wasn't even a bad person, you treated her well, it was just the smack. You know you can't bring up a child with that about them.

You can't beat yourself up your whole life. Your father was an evil bastard, you made big mistakes but you've taken responsibility. I know it ain't easy for you but you can't keep tormenting yourself every single day.

She reminds me of mum, Jean. She looks like her too. Quiet, caring but scared of the person that has had a hold over her her whole life. I don't blame mum, dad was mental, there was something wrong with his head. He never wanted me, he only cared about my sister and he took out whatever it was that was wrong with him on me and mum. I still used to sneak back and see her after he threw me out on my 16th birthday, but I suppose I still blamed her in some way. Going to see Jean is a bit like some kind of therapy, like I'm making up for giving up on mum. Or did she give up on me?

"You are careful out there ain't ya love? I worry about you."

"You know I am Jean, you don't have to worry about me. How you been? How's he been?"

"He's hardly here anymore, goes to the pub in the morning and comes back late at night, don't really talk to me, I prefer it that way. I'm okay, same as always."

"You could run away with me, hahaha!"

"I'll be here for the rest of my life, nothing will change, I've made my peace with that. You can still change though."

"I'll always be running Jean, she'll never come and find me now, wherever I go it will always follow me, at least here I've got you."

"I won't be around forever, love."

"We'll see."

"Look at me, I'm nearly 70, my husband don't talk to me, the only thing I have to be grateful for is that he don't knock me about anymore. That's how it's been for nearly 40 years. You're waiting for something that's never going to happen."

She's right ain't she? I am waiting for something that probably will never happen. I live off that hope though, how can I let go of the last thing that's keeping me going? I can't. I don't know how to stop beating myself up, telling myself I'm worthless. That's what dad did and then I went and proved him right. I've changed, well I've changed some things, if I gave up the hope I'd just go back to what I was, there'd be no point anymore. I don't have anyone else, at least I'd end up on my own, that wouldn't be so bad.

Time to go and get ready for work. I say goodbye to Jean, I leave her sitting at her kitchen table, she probably keeps sitting there until he comes back. That's what mum used to do, just sat there waiting for the person who made her life a misery, looking at the clock, becoming more and more quiet as it got nearer the time he'd be back. The kids are still playing downstairs, the nights are longer now, there's a couple of people arguing on the floor below, I hate the sound of people shouting. I see that silly cow coming home from work, she turns her head as I pass her, same sneer on her face.

Why do you still do it? You've done everything else to change your life but you're holding onto the one thing that degrades you most. You can walk away from it if you want, you ain't stupid. Imagine if she ever did come and find you and then found out how you still make your living. How do you think she'd feel about that? You talk about wanting to make changes, you made the biggest one, you stopped the drugs, but you won't stop doing this? I don't think you really do

want to walk away from it, you live your life on a loop, every
day is just a repeat of the last. The only person to blame for
that is yourself.

It's dark, the street is badly lit, there's the canal just behind it, probably quite easy to murder someone and then dump a body in there, I reckon you'd get away with it. It's turned cold, it was warm earlier. There's another girl on the other side of the road. I wonder if she is looking over and thinking the same or is she thinking what's that old woman still doing out here. She's skinny, I used to look like that, unhealthy skinny, legs that look like they'd snap if she fell in a certain way. No matter how many vegetables I eat, I ain't ever gonna look like that again. Not that I want to.

It's starting to rain, this is fucking shit. If I walked into a shop and took an application form, would I ever hear back from them? Would I end up like that bitter cow that works on the tills? Sometimes I think it's the danger that keeps me going. That counsellor might be right too though, I just don't want to let go of this last part of my past. I'm holding on to that one last thing because I don't think I'm worth a complete change. Could just be a load of psychobabble nonsense too. Or is that just an excuse?

There's a car coming, you only drive down here at night for one thing, unless you're lost, but you ain't really going to get lost down here. It slows down as it reaches the skinny girl, whoever is in it will be eyeing her up, looking at those skinny legs. I hope he doesn't like her. Or do I? I think I want her to get in the car. I don't want to do this anymore do I? Why not? I always thought I never cared enough. The image of the kids playing in the playground, the little girl sitting next to me and crying, they flash through my head.

The car drives on, the girl is still standing on the street. The car pulls up next to me, I've never taken much notice of the people inside the car before, they're just a person, you look through everything, you just get on with it. I can't do that now though, he's a good looking man, young, younger than me anyway. He doesn't look nervous, like he knows what he's doing. His eyes, they don't seem to have any depth to them, there's something not right. Is he married? Why the fuck am I having a moral crisis right now? I need money to survive.

He drives off, didn't say a word, just stared and went. What am I doing? Another car is coming. It stops by the other girl. I don't want to do this do I? What the fuck is wrong with me tonight. She gets into the car and it drives off. Fuck it, I can't do it anymore, I've had enough. What if Claire did come and find me, I don't think she ever will but if she did, what would she think? I can't even admit to myself what I do, I wrap it up in words like 'work' and 'shifts'. I sell my body and I don't really want to, what do I get from it? Nothing.

You've broken the cycle. Well, you've broken part of it. You need to break the rest of it. You can't keep sitting down in that little park every morning, you're just tormenting yourself, watching and waiting. It's the last part that you have to break, you need to walk past it keep on going until you get home. It'll hurt, you'll feel like you've betrayed her but you have to let go and live the rest of your life. You might think you don't deserve it, but you do, you've changed your life, what you did was in the past, at least make the rest of it happy.

Do I put it back on the wall or not? I don't really want to but that counsellor woman said I should do, learn to love myself she says. I'm not ready for that yet. I might buy a new one, Jean lent me some money, I have no idea where she got it from but when I told her that I walked away the other night, that I'm never going to go and stand on that street ever again she gave it to me. She says I need to go, go and live somewhere else, I haven't got anywhere to go though, I've no proper money either. We'll see, like I always say, there's hope.

I'm going to do it for the last time today, I want to sit in that park one more time. I know she ain't going to come back and find me but I'll feel better if I do it this one last time. Closure, that's the word. There aren't any kids down there this morning, they must have gone back to school. It'll be easier if they ain't about. Go on I'll have a look in the mirror, if she turned up I'd want to know what she's going to see! A tired old woman it looks like, maybe getting a new mirror won't be such a good idea.

This shouldn't be a big thing, all I'm doing is changing a habit, but I'm shaking, I feel a bit dizzy. The bench is cold, why have I been doing this for so long? Every single day for 15 years. I've wasted my life, punishing myself over and over for mistakes I made a long time ago, being scared to let go of the mistakes I made. At least the sky is blue, it's not one of them dreary, cold days that makes me feel a lot worse. You can dream one more time though can't you? Allow yourself to be taken away and feel all those good feelings, see things you'll never see again?

We're there, together, me pushing her on the swing, her laughing, telling me to push her higher. The best thing that ever happened to me. When she gets off the swing she hugs me, I pick her up and we walk over to the bench, I sit down still holding her, start to tell her a story about princesses and castles, she listens, closing her eyes imagining she's there in the story. When it's finished we get up and walk away together, holding hands, up the stairs where I put her to bed, kissing her on her forehead, standing at the door watching her as I leave the room. I fucked it all up, but at least she's probably had a better life, goodbye sweetheart, I won't be waiting here anymore.

"Goodbye, mummy."

I turn around, it's the little girl that was in the park the other day. She's saying goodbye to her mum as she goes off somewhere with her dad. I thought it was her. Time to leave it all behind now. I deserve better than this.

Jules and Giles

It really is so quaint around here. When I told all my friends that I was going to buy myself a flat on the Shakespeare Estate they all said I was crazy. They'll eat you for breakfast, I give it two months and you'll be trying to sell it again. I shouldn't expect anything less from them really, good people but they don't know what it's like to live in the real world. All they know are the suburbs and small little villages where they can stick to themselves, drinking Pimms and gin and tonics. That life is not for me, I want to see how people really live.

It's a lovely little flat, look out my window and you can see out across the city, I chose it because it's so high up, gives a dramatic effect, do you know what I mean? It's hard to explain to people that don't understand. The people as well, they're lovely, a bit rough around the edges but I've been trying to introduce a few friends to the area, add a bit of culture to it. A few juice bars and organic food shops wouldn't go amiss. I've started a little vegetable plot on the roof of my block, going to try and see if I can get a few people interested in urban gardening.

I do love going for a walk around. These large concrete buildings, so many different people inside them from all walks of life. I must admit some of them do seem as though they are quite poor, large amount of immigrants too, not that immigrants bother me, I think it's great, languages and cultures should be learned. I went on a gap year after 6th form to Tanzania to teach poor children, such a unique experience and something I can put on the old C.V if my forays into the business world don't work out too well.

When I finished university father said he would help me with the deposit to buy a nice little flat down near the docks. I told him that I didn't want to live by the docks, far too boring, all the people there are so plain, they all do the same thing. When I told him that I was going to be moving here he wasn't best pleased, he gave me the money but he still hasn't come and visited, I have to go home each month. I do think he would love it if he gave it a chance, he could sit on the roof with a cigar and a G & T.

I've had to try and butter him up a bit recently, I've got a bit of business proposition. There's a flat a couple of doors down that's for sale. I've been talking to my friend Giles and we have both came to the conclusion that what would be really great around here is a juice bar, all organic of course, we can grow the veg on the roof. The thing is, we want to get some locals involved, I mean we're local now too, well I am, but someone really local, you know? Someone that has grown up around here and would like to get involved in the juice bar business.

I put an advert in the local paper but there hasn't been too much in the way of replies, I really did think we'd be inundated! Giles says he has a friend that lives in the block opposite, not sure how he met this friend, seems a bit cagey when I ask him, but who cares? If this guy wants to put a bit of money into our venture it would be great. It'd be lovely for him to be the face of Jules and Giles' Juice Bar. Great name, I came up with it myself, it has a really catchy ring to it. Our other friend Vaughn wants to look after the garden so we're thinking Vaughn's Vegetables.

God I hope this guy gets involved. We've got a meeting with him this morning and I'm really nervous. It could be the start of something amazing, I'd really feel like I'm giving something back. I don't usually wear a suit but I've put one on today, trying to look the part. Giles has said he would already be there waiting for me. He lives over at the docks but he spends an awful lot of time around here. Strange fellow, I met him one day when I went to Cheltenham with my ex-girlfriend, we've been friends ever since. He likes a flutter on the old gee gees, God only knows how much money he's lost.

Bloody Jules, why he wants to open this God forsaken juice bar I will never know. What is it with people of culture and class deciding they want to take over these deprived areas? They really don't understand that the people don't really want them there. If you ask me they should just level the whole fucking estate, probably better if the people were still in it too. People like Jules could open as many juice bars and health food shops as they want then. He is so naïve, I suppose if he's happy then it can't do any harm.

I have to introduce him to this bloody Mr E or Big E or whatever his name is. Not a very nice character, reminds me of one of those villains you see on the television. Bit of a caricature, I don't think he's half as frightening as he thinks he is, saying that he'd probably have no qualms in disposing of me and Jules at the bottom of a river. He does have a rather interesting business proposition though, I can't let Jules in on it, but he doesn't need to know, he'll be quite happy selling juice and thinking he's creating the new Hampstead.

Take a deep breath Jules, this could be the big one. I knock on the door confidently, to my surprise Jules opens it. He's not looking too business like, very casual, shorts and flip flops, he looks like he should be on the beach in the Bahamas. He leads me into a living room where there is an enormous man sitting on an armchair. Not enormous as in fat but very well built. Not the kind of man I'd like to get on the wrong side of, I'm sure I've seen him about somewhere before.

"Jules, this is Big E, Big E this is Jules the man that wants to open a juice bar."

"Nice to meet you Mr E. You have no idea how much I've been looking forward to meeting you today, it's such an opportunity, one we could all benefit from. Our problem is…"

"Woah, slow down. I've already come to an arrangement with your friend Giles here. Whatever it is you need, I'll provide it."

"Well you see it's not really money that we're after…"

"I'll protect the business too."

"Protection? Whatever for?"

"I think you should have a word with Giles. Now if you two would excuse yourselves, I've got some things to sort out."

Well that was quick, I was expecting a long drawn out business meeting where I lay out my proposal, seems as though this Big E character is pretty decisive, little hesitation, just the man that we need. I do wonder what Giles said to him though? I must probe him further about how he actually got to know this individual.

"What kind of a man is Mr E, Giles?"

"Just the kind of man we need to get this business up and running, don't worry about him, he'll provide us with the money, you won't have to ask your father."

"Yes, but what I wanted Giles was someone that grew up here, lived and breathed the place, could be the face of Giles and Jules' Juice Bar."

"He said he'd find someone. For God's sake Jules stop worrying, it'll all be splendid. You can have your bloody juice bar and I can make some money."

"You are part of it too, I wouldn't like to think you're going to take a backseat."

"No, no, no, of course I won't. I've got to fly Jules old boy, need to see a man about a dog as they say around here, hahaha!"

Well that really was rather simple. Didn't need too much input from Jules, I thought he'd say something ridiculous and ruin the whole thing. He's still none the wiser about the other business proposition, he might have actually liked a bit of danger but I can't trust him, the man is an idiot. Not to say I don't like him, I do, I think he's a lovely fellow, comes from very good stock, he's just an idiot. Vaughn is also an idiot and I don't like him, in fact I'd be rather happy if that E chap disposed of him and those fucking vegetables, I need him though, he does know what he's doing when it comes to growing things.

I can't wait to get away from here. I have a tip for the big race, now I have a few pounds I might have a bit of a flutter.

Nothing too big, just for interest. When this is all up and running I might buy myself a horse, there's a man I know that says he has a few. I wonder if Mr E would like to have some involvement with a horse? He looks like the kind of man that you'd see in the bookies. I'll have to ask him next time.

There it is, we've done it, Giles and Jules' Juice Bar. It's a little bit hard to find but business is absolutely thriving, I can't believe how well we've done in the first few weeks. The most encouraging thing is that there are so many local people coming to the bar. We've actually expanded a little bit, Vaughn has a vegetable plot on the roof and he also has another one somewhere else, he's very secretive about it, says that the way he grows the vegetables is some kind of special technique and only he is allowed to go to the other plot.

I've not seen that Big E chap since either, the money has all been there though. I'd have thought a man would want to come and see the business that he's put so much money into. I must say, I didn't expect to have the kind of clientele that we do, lots of teenagers and young men. I did want to get the locals involved but I thought we might be able to attract a little higher class of clientele. I suppose I can't complain but I am a little suspicious as to why there are so many young people coming here and ordering kale juice.

See, look at this fellow standing drinking a juice, it's rather bizarre. His jeans are falling down around his legs, I don't quite know how he manages to keep them up, one of them funny looking scarf things around his head and when he speaks he sounds so uncouth. Yet here he is with a quinoa and kale juice in his hand. Oh well, beggars can't be choosers I suppose, we're making vast amounts of money and I'm having friends ask about other business opportunities that might arise in the area. I'm thinking a health food shop or even a vitamin store.

"Hi, I'm Jules, lovely to meet you, so glad you've decided to come to our juice bar. How's the juice? I do love a bit of quinoa myself."

"Yeah, it's not bad still, this is your juice bar? I thought it was my man Giles's. Why do you posh boys live around here anyway?"

"Oh no! Giles doesn't live around here, I do though. I've always wanted to live in the 'hood! I'm joking, it's an up and coming area, in a few years it'll be amazing!"

"……. Yeah, anyway, nice juice, hope the extras are better."

That's funny, I hope Giles isn't giving away free things on the side, I wouldn't put it past him to give out free vegetables. I am ever so proud of us all though, we've all worked so hard to get this place up and running, it really is a dream come true. Looking up at that small sign with the name on it I honestly feel like crying. It was never about the money for me, it was always about giving something back to the community that I lived in, becoming part of it, accepted, being one of these people at long last.

I've got myself into quite a situation here. Mr E wants nothing to do with horses and I've promised a man a large sum of money. I'm thinking about burning down that fucking juice bar, if Mr E won't get on board with my ideas then I'll teach him a lesson, he needs to know his place in the grand scheme of things. When Jules gets the insurance money I'll be entitled to some of it. It's not the ideal way to go about it, the juice bar has been doing really rather well.

I need to do something about that fucking Vaughn too. He's been trying to blackmail me, telling me that he's not getting paid enough and that if I don't give him more money he's going to tell Jules what's going on. I've been thinking Mr E should take care of that one, however it might be better to deal with it myself. He doesn't seem like a particularly careful man. I might pay one of the local scoundrels to make it look like Vaughn fell in the canal. I am clever aren't I? I am wasted really, I can't wait to get out of all this nonsense.

I've been searching for Giles for days, he's just completely disappeared, I even went to Big E's flat but no one opened the door, I'm sure there was someone inside though. Since he's gone missing people have stopped turning up at the juice bar, only a couple of luvvies from Kensington. Why the hell has he gone missing now? I knew I should have never trusted him, I like Giles but the man is utterly unreliable, he's probably gambled half our money away on the 3.30 at Towcester. Vaughn doesn't know where he is either, he's been neglecting his plot and I am having to buy things at the local supermarket. Not that anyone is buying anyway.

Funny thing happened on the way home from the shop yesterday, I was followed by a car all the way back to the estate. Two men were inside, I felt rather uncomfortable but I can't for the life of me think why someone would be following me. I've just had to go on a trip up to the west end as I needed a few ingredients that you can't really get around here. I've started a special promotion that I am hoping will bring all the customers back.

Those bloody kids wanted nothing to do with making Vaughn end up in the canal so I'm going to do it myself. I'm waiting for him now. It's bloody dark down here, I feel like I'm in some Victorian drama, amongst the great unwashed, what was that painting? Gin Lane! That wasn't Victorian though was it Giles? You're not quite as clever as you used to be. Anyway, all I have to do is get Vaughn drunk and then push him the canal, they'll think he fell in and I'll be in the clear.

"Vaughn old boy! Join me, we'll have a few drinks and sort this horrid mess out. I chose the canal because I thought it was rather atmospheric, we can pretend we're a couple of people that live on that bloody housing estate that Jules lives on."

Good God, today has been the worst day of my life. The juice bar is gone! I woke up this morning at about 5am because there was a commotion outside, people shouting and banging. I went outside to find firemen putting out a fire in the juice bar. The whole place has gone up in flames, it's completely beyond repair. I still can't get hold of Giles, he's disappeared off the face of the earth, none of our friends have seen him or even have any idea where he might have got himself off to, I really need him right now.

To make things worse that Big E chap turned up at my door demanding money, far more money than we had ever agreed on. He was quite menacing, talking about throwing me in the canal if I didn't cough up the money, said nobody would ever find me. Where does Giles meet these people and why must he get mixed up in business deals with them. He could have found a nice chap that wouldn't bring us any trouble. I have to be honest though, I am a bit scared. I know the insurance will pay some money but not how much he wants. Fucking Giles!

I suppose I could just pack up and go, borrow a few quid from father, I could go back to Tanzania, or some other place in

Africa even Asia. Things haven't quite turned out how I would have like here, it's very quickly losing its appeal, my juice shop has been burned down, my friend has gone missing and now a rather large, threatening man called Big E is going to throw me in the canal. I'm not sure I am up for all this, perhaps my friends were right, this place is the pits, God why did I ever come here, why did I ever think I could fit in?

Giles is dead! He was pulled out from the canal last night. This has turned into a complete fucking catastrophe. The man is dead! I really don't understand what has happened. The police said they suspect foul play but why would anyone want to hurt poor Giles! I thought perhaps he had racked up a gambling debt and then thrown himself in the canal because he couldn't pay, he was a bit melodramatic but that's obviously not the case if the police think someone has hurt him. God this could all be my fault!

Well, I am hanging upside down in some kind of a garage. I'm not really sure where I am, some men came to the door this morning barged in and put some kind of a bag over my head and now I find myself here. I'll take an educated guess that it has something to do with this Big E fellow, problem is I don't have his money, insurance won't pay out straight away and they're saying the fire was suspicious anyway. He really is going to have to wait until then, there's no need to get so bloody aggressive about the whole situation.

I am confident that I'm not going to end up like Giles, he needs me. One thing that I'd forgotten about was Vaughn, he's gone missing too. Last night I went to look at the vegetable plot and it doesn't look like it has been tended to at all. I didn't like the guy, if he ends up in the bottom of the canal too I won't be too bothered. Surely they would have disposed of him and Giles together? I'll have to ask this Big E chap what has happened because I really am in the dark here and it has absolutely nothing to do with me.

There are a few nasty looking tools on table from what I can see from here, the old vision isn't too good when you're upside down though. I hope they come back soon so we can reach an amicable agreement and I can go home.

"Where are the drugs?"

"What bloody drugs? What are you talking about?"

"Your friend Giles was selling drugs from your lovely little juice bar, now he's dead and I want my money and my drugs back."

"Bloody Giles! I knew there would have to be something dodgy involved! I have no idea where your drugs are, I didn't even know he was selling drugs there!"

"You really are that stupid?"

"Obviously...."

"I'm going to let you go, you are to go and get me my money and my drugs back. What about that other fella that was in it with you? Vince or Vance or whatever his fucking name was."

"Vaughn? He's disappeared."

"What is it with you posh people and disappearing? I'm not sure I should let you go."

"If you don't let me go I can't help you. Whatever happened to Giles?"

"I don't know, it had nothing to do with me, why would I have wanted him dead? He had my money. He came round last week talking about a horse and how it'd be a good investment for me. I told him I wanted nothing to do with horses and the next thing I know they find him at the bottom of the canal."

"Well I'm afraid Mr E old fellow we're in quite a pickle. I just want to go home, you want your money back and Giles is dead. I would appreciate it if you could let me down?"

"If you don't get my money back you'll be hanging there again and next time I'll be using those tools on you. Don't fuck me about Jules."

I do wonder what ever happened to that Mr E chap. He's probably still on that accursed housing estate, taking money off people and selling drugs. I was convinced that he killed Giles but it appears not, the police arrested him and then let him go. I've no idea how Giles ended up in that canal, it really was all rather odd. Perhaps it had something to do with a horse or some other nonsense. Quite frankly I don't care. The man used me and I could very well have ended up in prison, I don't think I would have lasted very long in a prison.

It's all behind me now anyway, sitting here on the beach in Thailand. The day that E fellow let me go I fled, I explained the whole situation to father and even though he was a bit miffed he gave me some money and told me to flee the country. Another funny coincidence was I met Vaughn out here! Is nice to see a familiar face. He didn't say much about all that funny business, I suspect he was as miffed as I am. He really has done rather well for himself somehow, absolutely rolling in money. I've learned my lesson, I shan't be interfering in places that I shouldn't anymore. Vaughn was talking about opening a massage parlour, probably not my thing though is it?

Rats

Look at them, lying there out of their heads, they don't even know what planet they're on. The state of this place as well. There's rubbish everywhere, the toilet's broken and it fucking stinks. They're like rats, all sticking together until one of them robs another and they start fighting. There's syringes on the floor too, I don't know why I come here, I'll end up getting AIDS one day. I spit on one of them that's lying on an old crusty sofa with holes in it, I'd throw a match on it if they weren't giving me money every day, he doesn't move, doesn't even notice. Little rats.

There's a couple of kids hanging round by the car, I tell them to fuck off. They run off quickly. There's another kid standing by the door to one of the flats, I know his mum. The kid looks at me like he wants to kill me, I give him a smile and he looks down at the floor. I haven't seen his mum in a while come to think of it, I wonder what she's up to. She better not be scoring off someone else, I'll have to put a stop to that, ain't no one round here getting in the way of my business, most of them are just little scrotes that think they're big men.

I feel bad for scaring the kid. I don't know why but I do. Usually I don't have feelings like that, I don't care about anyone except for me and my daughter and sometimes the wife. He didn't choose to have the life that he has and there ain't anything that he can do about it. What can I do though? That's just the way it's turned out for him, some of us have good lives, others don't. He's the same age as my little one. I don't like feeling like this, I hate emotion, I can't have it, if I felt bad for people I wouldn't be able to do what I do.

Oh well fuck it, I need to go and get the dough off of this geezer who owes me money otherwise he might start thinking he's got away with it. I grew up round here but it's different these days, fucking junkies taking over the place, I'm glad I don't live here no more but I do miss it in a way. People say living on top of each other is bad but it ain't really, you get to know people, well you used to, it ain't really like that no more. A lot of fucking immigrants as well these days, wouldn't let my daughter grow up here. Lucky I'm loaded hey? The state of some of these blocks, anyone would think animals lived in them.

Another flat and another load of junkies, there's one of them in this place that I like though, always have done, he's never caused me no trouble. I don't know how he's ended up here because he seems like he's quite clever. I asked him once but he just laughed, usually I wouldn't let someone get away with that but I just let it go. He doesn't even look like a junkie, he wears nice clothes, doesn't look skinny either, most of them don't eat. There's got to be some back story to this geezer, I'll have to find out.

"Why do you live here with all these?"

"I'm a smackhead, I spend all my money on gear, where else am I going to live?"

"Yeah but you don't look like you're form round here…"

"I'm not, but I've ended up here."

"Why can't you get some money off your old man or something?"

"He doesn't speak to me, anyway if he gave me money it'd be going straight to you and not getting me out of here. I don't even dislike it here, the residents probably don't like me though."

"I reckon you should go and see him then!"

Posh cunt, who does he think he is? I thought he was alright but he ain't, he's just the same as the rest of them, he probably lives here just because he thinks it's cool, he should be living up in Chelsea or something, I reckon he's telling me lies, I'll have to watch him. His looks healthy, almost like he ain't even on gear, if I didn't sell it to him I wouldn't believe he was a smackhead. I might just rob him next time he wants something, he's gotta be loaded, I ain't having it that he ain't. Anyway fuck him, where's this other fucker I've come looking for?

"Where's J?"

"In that room over there."

I kick the door open, I don't really need to do that, I just thought it'd be funny, shit him up a bit. The posh geezer jumps behind me when I do it. J is lying on the bed, he jumps up as he sees me. Little rat, if I didn't make so much money off him I'd hope he overdosed.

"Your money's in the drawer."

"It fucking better be or I'll throw you out that window."

"It's there, just take it."

It's there. I wouldn't really have thrown him out the window, that would have been stupid. Got to keep them in check though ain't ya? I count the money, the little rat sitting on the mattress on the floor looking up, shaking as I count it. Surprised he's even got a chest of drawers, it's the only piece of furniture in here. I push it over as I'm leaving, it makes a thudding sound as it hits the floor. He'll probably leave it there. The posh boy is sitting on the floor against the wall of the living room, he don't take no notice of me this time. He should be taking notice, who does he think he is?

"See this money? That's real money, I bet your old man don't walk around with bundles of cash like this. You boys should clean up the flat, you might catch AIDS in here."

"Fuck off."

"I'm in a good mood, don't you ever say anything like that to me again you little cunt. I'll cut you up so badly your parents won't know who you are."

"Yeah, yeah..."

Cheeky bastard. Who does he think he is? He'll be waiting a long time next time he's on the phone looking for something, I bet that will be in a few hours. I'll teach him a lesson, fuck it I'll give him some of that gear that I've got that's got rat poison in it. Ain't nobody that can talk to me like that. Don't he understand who I am? I should just go back in there and do him now, the bad gear would be easier though, it'll just look like he overdosed, just another dead junkie, no one gives a fuck about them anyway.

Time to go home for a bit. Get out of this shit hole. You know what? I am too good for this place. I know I grew up here but I am passed all that, outgrew it, I've become someone and I don't deserve to be living somewhere like this. I can see my old flat, where mum brought me and my brother up, we used to run around down here on the grass while she watched from the balcony. The door is still red, I can almost see her still standing on that balcony looking down at me and Sam. Everyone thought we were good boys, well he was, still is. Good job, nice house. Never comes and sees me though, thinks he's too fucking good for us. I make more money in a day than he does in a month.

My house is one of them out in the suburbs, they all look the same. Whether it's Wembley or Eltham, they just look the same. I can't stand the neighbours, they're always moaning that we're too loud when me mates are about. Stuck up old bastards, need putting down. I'd put a brick through the window but they'd just phone the Old Bill and I can't be doing with them coming around here. I've been thinking about taking Annie and the wife to Spain, retiring, I don't need to do all this no more, dealing with all these scum bags.

"Daddy!"

"Hello sweetheart! How's your day been? What did you do at school?"

"I painted a picture of a giraffe and I wrote your name on it! Do you want to see it?"

"Of course I do love, just give me five minutes while I talk to your mother and then you can show me what you've done."

She's my life, Annie. Sometimes I think she's the only thing that keeps me going. Money, it don't mean fuck all when compared to her. I've sent her to a private school, I want her to do the best she can. I remember the first day that she went in the doors of the school, I cried my eyes out, me the big man from the Shakespeare Estate. The only thing in the world that can make me cry. My heart becomes softer when I'm around her. I don't hate everyone and everything. You know what? I don't think I'll give that kid the gear with the rat poison in it, he's just a mouthy kid.

"How's she been?"

"She's fine, she's always fine, stop worrying about her so much."

"Of course I'm going to fucking worry about her, what's the matter with you."

"Oh shut up Eric, you might be able to frighten those junkies but you're not a big man in this house. I'm telling you that I'm perfectly able to look after her too and don't need you checking up and questioning me every time you get home."

"I was just asking..."

"Go and see the drawing she's done for you, she hasn't stopped going on about it since we've got home."

Fucking hell, I was only asking. She does like to get on her high horse that woman. If I'm honest I'm only with her because of Annie, I'd thought about leaving her before I found out she was pregnant. I ain't sure I can trust her, she knows too much about me, ain't many people that can say that. If I take them to Spain she might do me a favour and fuck off with some Spanish waiter called Jose. She had the cheek to call me a plastic gangster the other day, said I was full of shit and everyone knows it. Lucky she's a woman. See? She's making me angry now, I was in a good mood a few minutes ago.

Annie is sitting in the living room watching some cartoon on the television, there's some bear dancing and she's copying it. Not many things make me smile but watching her now is. I reckon she could be a dancer one day, be in one of them big theatres up in the west end. I don't understand all that theatre bollocks but she's going to be cleverer than me. I sit down on the sofa behind her, she turns around and runs over to her schoolbag and takes out a picture of a giraffe, daddy is written above it.

"That giraffe me?"

"Yeah, he's tall like you, he's nice too, just like you, daddy."

"Haha, you think daddy's nice?"

"Yeah! Are you going to come and pick me up from school tomorrow?"

"Yes, I promise I'll come and pick you up from school."

"Yay! Are you going out again today?"

"I don't think so, babe. Maybe later when you're asleep."

"Okay, wait until I'm asleep! I don't like it when you go out."

I'll ignore any phone calls tonight, the dirty junkies can sweat it out a bit, it'll be good for them. They deserve to feel a bit sick after they've been running around nicking stuff all day. It annoys me that they think they can phone me up whenever they like and I'm supposed to come running. They need to know that I'm the one that's in control. Looking at Annie and then thinking about having to go and mix with people that should be put down makes my stomach turn, going from looking at someone so perfect to a bunch of animals.

The phone's ringing and it's that little rat J, I certainly ain't breaking my promise for him. Annie's looking up at me, I can see it in her eyes that she's begging me not to answer the phone. I ain't gonna answer it. She's never asked me what I do, I wonder where she thinks I go? Does she think I go out and work like a mug like all the kids' dads at her school? Probably, she must know her dad ain't a mug. I don't want her to know though, she'd only worry about me. She doesn't know what I'm really like does she?

"Daddy...?"

"Yeah...?"

"Where do you go?"

"I just go and see some friends, they give me money."

"Why?"

"They like me a lot so they give me money."

"Do you hurt them?"

What the fuck?

"No, I don't hurt anyone, Annie, why do you ask that?"

"I saw a bad man on the television, people gave him money and sometimes he hurt them."

"Why you watching things like that?"

"I don't know…"

"Don't be watching things like that. I don't hurt anyone."

I do though don't I? Even when they give me the money I'm hurting them because they're putting shit in their veins or smoking rocks mixed with shit. What's all this about? Why am I thinking like this? It's their choice, they're the ones that are fucking up their own bodies, nothing to do with me. Their mothers and fathers should have brought them up better, looked after them like I look after Annie. It makes me angry to think that people think I am hurting anybody, I ain't, I'm just doing a job.

Phone's ringing again. It's that posh kid, I don't even know his name, the phone just flashes up 'Posh Kid'. I want to answer it, there's something about him but I can't work out what is. I'd never, ever let someone get away with talking to me the way he did.

"Yeah?"

"You about?"

"No, I ain't."

"I've got a proposition for you…"

"Who the fuck do you think you are? I own you, you don't ring me up making propositions to me…"

"I've acquired a very large sum of money…"

"And…"

"I thought you might be interested in my business proposition…"

"I don't do business with smackheads…"

"Really? How come you spend so much time around here then? Annie really would be disappointed."

"…."

"Speechless are we? Meet me at the flat in an hour."

"I'll kill you."

"No, you won't kill me, you will come though. Make sure you say goodnight to Annie before you leave."

How the fuck does he know anything about Annie? I'm gonna kill him. I'll throw him and his mate out the fucking window.

"I thought you weren't going out daddy?"

"I just have to go out for a little bit, something important has happened."

She turns away and ignores me. I hate it when she does that. I can't let him take liberties with me though, one starts and they all start. I want to know how he knows about Annie as well. I swear to God if he goes anywhere near her. I'm going to enjoy this, I was going to poison the little fucker but now I'm going to make it nice and slow. I might do his mate first and make him watch, let him know what's coming. His rich man daddy won't be able to pay to bring him back to life. He must be ill, how did he think he could talk about Annie and get away with it?

The door is open, I was going to kick it in anyway. They're both sitting down on the floor, the posh kid smiles as I walk into the room. He's really taking the piss now, he don't know what he's getting involved in. The other one doesn't even seem to notice that I've arrived, that's more annoying than him smiling. The door slams behind me, I look back and

160

there's another geezer standing there that I've never seen before. What the fuck is going on here?

"What the fuck is this? You're pushing my patience."

"Don't mind him, he's a friend of mine. He's been very eager to meet you."

I'm starting to feel a bit uncomfortable here. I ain't in control. I don't know who this other geezer is, he don't look like them, he definitely ain't a smackhead, I can see that.

"Who are you?"

"Don't worry about names, Eric. I know yours, you don't need to know mine. You used to know someone that I knew. She meant a lot to me but she isn't around anymore. Do you know why?"

"How the fuck would I know? Why would I even care?"

"You sold her bad gear. You knew about it too didn't you?"

"Listen mate, you're well out of your depth here, you do know who I am don't you?"

"You're Eric Jones, you grew up on this estate. You think you're a big time gangster, whereas the reality is that you're not. You sell drugs to kids, you're a bully, most people around here despise you, they wouldn't piss on you if you were on fire. Dreams of moving to Spain too haven't you? Oh, and little Annie. The poor girl is going to have to grow up knowing that her father likes to poison kids. Amazing what you can learn by standing outside a school and pretending to be a parent. Your wife talks too much by the way. Nice woman though."

"The three of you...."

"You're not threatening me, you might scare the pair of them but I'm well out of your league, Eric. The girl you poisoned, she was my sister. I'm going to make you pay for that."

"You two are fucking dead. As for you..."

"I told you, don't threaten me."

Bang! The fella drops down on the floor in front of me. I turn around to the two, the posh kid is holding a gun. The fucking idiot has tried to shoot me and missed and shot this other geezer that was going on and on about some fucking girl and me poisoning her. He's still holding the gun up, pointing it towards me now but I can see he's shitting himself, he

162

doesn't know what to do. His mate has fallen down against the wall. He's crying, this is fucking madness, how have I ended up in this situation?

"I never asked you your name? You know mine's Eric."

"Don't worry about my fucking name! Give me your money!"

"I didn't bring any with me, you called me out on short notice. This is all a bit silly ain't it? That poor geezer is dead, you don't really know how to use that either do you? We don't want anyone else getting hurt. Besides, I bet someone heard that gunshot, it'd be best if we all left here. I'm just going to walk out the door, forget it all happened. That's a good idea ain't it?"

"Shut the fuck up! I'm the one with the fucking gun. If you have no money, give me your drugs."

"I've only got a little bit on me."

"Give it to me then!"

Silly fucker, I was going to give it to him anyway. He'll be dead in a few hours. Just like this fucker on the floor and his sister.

"There you go."

The gun is still pointing at me, he's moving away towards the door. I ain't going to do nothing, it won't be hard to find him later, the old bill will probably find him first. The other one gets up and follows him, he can't look at me, he knows what the consequences of this will be.

"Just fucking shoot him, he'll find us."

The posh kid is almost at the door, he's thinking about it, I ain't sure, he looks like he might do it. His eyes don't look scared no more, they look down at the body then back at me. He has my life in his hands.

"I can't..."

"Well lets just fucking run then."

They both get to the door, turn and run, the door is wide open, the footsteps going down the stairs. I need to push the door to. I should get out of here but I want to know who this geezer on the floor is, there's no one around outside, I shut the door. I look in his pockets but I can't find nothing, he's wearing a suit, I didn't notice that before. This is fucking stupid, I'm going to get nicked for this, them two fuckers might phone the old bill themselves. There's nothing on him, who is he?

Fuck I need to go. Still no one outside, I shut the door again, me on the outside this time, down the stairs. I'm gonna get Annie and go. This is mad. I ain't even angry, I'm confused. I'm never confused. Phone's ringing, who the fuck is it now? It's the wife, what does she want, I tell her not to phone me, I'm in this situation because the silly bitch couldn't keep her mouth shut.

"What the fuck do you want?"

"Annie, she's in hospital..."

"What?"

"You left gear on the bedside table you fucking idiot, she ate it, the doctor doesn't think she's going to make it. What the fuck am I going to do? This is all your fault...."

Slumped against the wall. I never thought anyone could hurt me. She ain't going to make it, what the fuck did I do to deserve this?

The following is the first chapter from my upcoming novel Liar which will be released in September 2016. At the end of the extract there is a link to sign up so that you will be notified of its release and you will also receive two short stories a month for free. (If you signed up for this book there is no need to sign up again.)

Chapter 1

"Why don't you have a dad?"

"I do have a dad, he's just busy. He's going to come back one day and I'll bring him to school and then you'll all stop laughing at me. He's big and tall, he has a gun too, if you laugh at me he'll beat you all up."

I turn and run away to the sounds of laughter and my classmates imitating my voice. It doesn't happen all the time, only sometimes. When they are bored and want to pick on someone different they choose me. The rest of the time it's the fat kid whose clothes don't fit him properly. I'm thankful for the fat kid. If it wasn't for him it would be me all the time. I hope he never goes on a diet or his mum never wins some money. I sit in the corner of the playground and watch. Watch and wait until they forget they were picking on me.

They are right, I don't have a dad. I have never seen him, I don't even know what his name is. I don't want to admit that to them though. If admit it then they would tease me more. If I lie it might make them think, maybe some of them will believe me and be scared. Mum says that I shouldn't listen to what the other kids say. She says they are only jealous of me because I can tell such good stories. None of them want to listen to my stories though. If they only listened for ten minutes they would like them, they would stop teasing me then.

I hope mum hasn't gone out tonight. I have a new story that I want to tell her. She hasn't been home in the evenings for weeks, when she gets back I am already in bed asleep. I know we need the money but she spends it all anyway. If she isn't home tonight I'll just go and see the nice old lady that lives in the block next door. I wanted mum to be the first to hear it but I just can't keep it in anymore, if I don't tell someone I'll forget it. The other kids have started to tease the fat kid. I think it's safe to go back out onto the playground.

As I walk towards them I kick a stone that's lying on the floor. Pretending to be a football player. Pretending I am at

Wembley and about to score a goal in the cup final. One of the other kids comes over and joins me. He's not my friend but he doesn't tease me. He talks to me about football and what he does at the weekend. If none of the other kids see him, he sometimes walks back home with me after school. He lives on the floor above me. He said his mum doesn't want him to walk home with me but he doesn't care. Just don't let her see us together.

As we kick the stone back and forth he asks me what I am doing after school tonight. I tell him that I need to go home and see my mum. She's been busy working recently. I can see a smirk on his face as I say it. One of the other kids calls out to him and he runs off, leaving me to the stone and my imagination. The teacher told the old lady, Mrs Smith, that I have a vivid imagination. Mum was busy so she couldn't go to the parent's evening. Mrs Smith said she would go instead. I don't really know what a vivid imagination is. I do like to dream though, even when I'm awake I still try to dream.

Back in the classroom the teacher gives us some work. It's boring. I wish she would give us something exciting. If she gave us something exciting she wouldn't have to tell me off for daydreaming. I look around the classroom at all the other children. Some of them are sleeping and some of them are doing their work. The teacher isn't paying any attention. The fat kid is playing with his ruler. I sometimes wonder if one day he'll go crazy and kill us all. I hope he doesn't, maybe I should make friends with him. Then he might not kill me, just kill all the others.

The bell rings and the teacher lets us go. I run out the door as fast as I can, the quicker I get out the further away I am from the kids that walk the same way home as me. I look back and can't see any of them. I walk slower, if I get home too quickly mum might not be there, the later I am, the more chance there is that she'll be home. I wish she would take a holiday like some of the other kid's mums. I don't think she has ever taken a holiday. As I walk across the park our estate comes into view. I can see the windows to our flat. It doesn't look like anyone is home, I don't know why but just by looking at the windows I know if someone is inside or not.

Our estate is big. Big tall, long buildings. We live on the bottom floor so I can play football outside the door if mum is at home and busy with work. There are ten floors above us. I always wanted to live on one of the higher floors, if I lived on one of them I could look out across the city. I can't see anything from my window, only trees. The boy in my class who lives above me said at night you can see all the lights from the other buildings. I asked him if I could come up and see it some time but he said his mum doesn't allow anyone inside their house.

There is a park just outside the door too. We don't use it though. At night some of the older kids hang around there smoking and drinking. There is broken glass all over the floor. One of the little girls that lives next to Mrs Smith went in there one day and her hand got pricked by a needle. They had to take her to hospital. Mrs Smith said the needle could make her very sick. She has to wait for three months before she knows if she is okay. Now none of the other children will play with her. Even my mum said don't play with her and my mum doesn't care who I play with.

Next to the park there is a newspaper shop, an off license and a fish and chip shop. Sometimes when mum has some money she lets me go to the fish and chip shop to buy dinner. I buy a battered sausage and a large portion of chips. If I have enough money I buy a coke too. Mum sends me to the newspaper shop to buy her cigarettes, I am supposed to be 16 to buy them but the man doesn't care, he knows they are for mum. When he gives me the cigarettes he winks at me. I feel bad because sometimes I steal a chocolate bar when he turns round to get the cigarettes.

I've only been into the off license once. They only sell beer in there and the man wouldn't let me buy it for mum. He said if she wants it she'll have to come and get herself. I know he sells it to the other kids though. I see them at night when I am kicking the ball against the wall. I'm not sure why he doesn't like me. After that day I went home and wrote a story about the man and he got eaten by a lion. I told it to mum and she really liked that one. I hope she likes my new one, it doesn't have any lions but it has a dinosaur. Mrs Smith will definitely like it.

Our flat is right in the middle. There are nineteen on our floor and ours is number 9. Last year mum stopped working for a few months. She said she needed a rest. She painted the door red and put some flowers on the windowsill. When she went back to work I tried to keep the flowers alive but they died. I gave them water every day but it didn't seem to work. The door is dirty now too, one of the windows has some cardboard in the corner, someone throw a stone at it. I don't know why. I remember it frightened me. Mum said not to worry, it was an accident, I'm not sure it was though.

I open the door and call out. There is no reply. The house is empty. I look into mum's room to see if she has been home recently. Her clothes are all over the floor and I can smell her perfume. Her room is different from the rest of the flat. The walls are a dark pink colour. There is carpet on the floor too. It's clean, the clothes just making it look messy. There are mirrors on the wall and she has a lamp on the table next to her bed. I'm not allowed to go in but when she is out I always open the door to have a look.

The living room doesn't have much in it. There is one sofa, a wooden chair in the corner and a small table with the television on top. We used to have a coffee table in the middle but it disappeared one day. Mum said she threw it out because she didn't like it but I looked in the rubbish tip outside and couldn't see it. Maybe someone came and took it away. The floor has no carpet, only black tiles that are freezing cold in the winter, especially if she forgets to pay the electricity bill. Last year when she forgot I could see my breath in the air. I took some sheets from my bed and pretended I was on an expedition to the Antarctic to find some penguins.

My room is the smallest. I have my bed and a small wardrobe to keep my clothes in. There is no carpet in my room either. The walls are painted white, I want to paint them blue but mum says I'll have to wait until next year. Underneath my bed I keep some of the books that I stole from the library. I push them right into the corner so that she can't find them. Not that she comes in here anyway. Just in case, though. If she found out I was stealing books she would never let me go to the library again.

It's nearly summer time so the house isn't very cold. It doesn't get dark until very late either. When it doesn't get dark until late I can stay outside playing football for longer. I can stay at Mrs Smith's for longer too. She doesn't like me to walk back home in the dark. I'm not scared but she says some of the older kids might cause trouble and she is too old to walk back with me because she'd have to walk back on her own then. I think she doesn't want to see mum, but maybe she's right, it isn't very safe around here at night.

Looking out the window I see some of the other kids playing football. I really want to go out and play with them but they won't let me. They call me names and say bad things about my mum. Instead I just watch them from the window, hoping that they can't see me. Every time I watch them playing I hope they will stop playing and call out to me to come and join them. I can show them how good I am then, I could even tell them about myself, if they knew about me they wouldn't hate me anymore.

As the light begins to fade their mum's call out to them from the windows above. None of them wanting to hurry inside. If it was my mum calling me I would come in as quick as I could. They don't seem to care though, they see their mums all the time. I only see mine when she isn't busy at work and that's not often. When they've gone back inside I think about sneaking upstairs to one of the balconies and looking out over the city. I hear a loud bang from outside, one of the older kids is playing with a firework. I change my mind.

I think about the presentation that we have to do at school tomorrow. We have to think of a place that we'd really like to go to and describe it to the rest of the class. I still can't think of somewhere that I'd really like to go to. The teacher says it has to be real, I can't make it up. One of the books that I stole from the library is the Jungle Book. I'm not sure if it's real or not. Mrs Smith said it's in India but I don't believe that there are animals that talk in India. I think I will choose the jungle in India, I just won't talk about animals that talk, I can have animals though, especially tigers, I love tigers.

I don't know what the jungle looks like, I can only think of it as how I imagine. I close my eyes and pretend I am there in India. I can see really tall trees, the top is completely green, the sky is covered with only small bits of light coming through. It's hot, really hot. I am wearing only a t shirt and some shorts. Above me I can see monkeys swinging through the trees, screaming out loudly, telling all the other monkeys that there is a small nine year old boy walking through their jungle. They hold their babies close to their bodies as they swing through the trees.

In front of me there is a river. I can see a crocodile waiting. Patiently waiting for something to come along that it can eat. A small deer is next to the river drinking water. The top of the crocodile glides along the surface silently, the deer unable to see or hear him. As the crocodile is almost upon the deer one of the monkeys above lets out a loud screech and the deer turns and runs back into the green forest. The crocodile is angry that he has to wait longer to have his dinner. The monkeys above laughing to themselves having ruined the crocodile's plans.

Across the river I spot a tiger. She moves slowly through the forest, frightened of nothing. The monkeys stop laughing and swing back through the trees. The master of the forest has arrived and everyone is making way. From across the river she spots me, only looking briefly before carrying on her way. Not bothered about the strange, small boy walking through her home. Maybe she thinks I am not enough to eat, she wants something bigger. Even the crocodile has swam away. Away from the beautiful cat to find somewhere he can wait in peace, away from the monkeys too.

As the tiger walks off to find her dinner a large bird flies down from the trees and perches on a branch next to my head. A parrot. He looks at me with curiosity, his look asking what am I doing here. Am I lost? I shake my head in reply. He lets out a loud sqwuak and flies away again. It is so peaceful here. Only the sounds of the animals and the water flowing. I'm in a place where nobody can tease me. I wish I could wait here all the time, each evening I spend on my own waiting for mum to come home I wish it was here in this forest.

I jump to another loud bang. This time it's not a firework but the sound of the door closing. It has gotten dark without me noticing, mum has arrived home. I haven't turned any of the lights on so she probably thinks I am asleep. Her footsteps sound clumsy, as though she is tripping over. I know she isn't wearing her high heels because I saw them on the floor when I looked in her room. She goes into the kitchen and I hear the sound of her lighter. The same clicking sound for the next ten minutes. I quietly take off my clothes and slip underneath the covers of my bed. Hoping the door will open just a crack and she'll look in.

Another twenty minutes pass and there is still no sound from the kitchen. Maybe she is tired, sometimes she falls asleep on the kitchen table. I hear the sound of the chair moving against the floor and my heart jumps. Her footsteps get closer to my door and then stop just outside. The door opens slightly and I can just see her face from the light coming from outside. She is smiling, but her hands are shaky, the door wobbling slightly back and forth. I pretend to be asleep. I'm annoyed that she didn't come home in time for me to read her my story.

Silently she closes the door. I hear her footsteps go into her own room, the sound of her falling onto her bed. Tonight she is back early, I hope she will be awake in the morning. I want to tell her to take some time off, she looks tired lately. She won't listen to me but I can try. I drift off to sleep, flying back to the jungle that is my new safe place, where even the animals won't tease me or eat me. Where I don't have to wait each night for mum to come home. Where I don't have to pretend that I have a dad.

I've let him down, I know that. When I look in at him at night I know he's still awake, I can't bring myself to talk to him, what am I supposed say to him? I don't think he's as innocent as he makes himself out to be, surely he must know what's going on. The kids at his school, I knew all their mums when I was at school, they like to talk, but what else can I do? I can't take him out of school, he can't be hanging around here all day. Anyway, I want him to be at school, I want him to do well for himself, I can't have him ending up like me.

I am getting more and more tired of all of this. Standing around on lonely street corners every night, when I'm finished going to some manky old squat and then coming back home. What kind of life is this? It's no kind of life, if I was on my own I reckon I'd just end it all, but I couldn't do that to him, I might not give him the best life but it would be better than the life he'd have in some home or with some family that don't really care about him. I've tried to get out of this cycle before but I always fail, I don't know how to live any other way.

The road is dark, next to the old canal, the streetlights aren't all working, I'm used to it, I've forgotten what it feels like to be scared. Well scared like most people think, you know?

Scared of being murdered or raped, I don't ever get scared like that no more. What's the point? If I was I might as well stay at home and then we definitely wouldn't have anything to eat. When I say I'm scared, I'm scared of myself, scared of what I am doing to myself, scared of what I am doing to the boy, how is this all going to affect him when he's older?

At the end of the dark road I turn onto the high street, there ain't anyone about at this time of the night apart from a couple of homeless old boys. I suppose it could be worse, I could be one of them. I have something I can hold on to. The walk back every night is the worst part, the shame is all over me, my body constantly feels dirty, sometimes I walk back slower, just to make sure that he's not awake to see me come in the door. I know that's what he wants, but I can't face him, it's too difficult.

If his old man had stayed around I wonder if it would have all of turned out like this? I doubt it, I wouldn't have to do what I do. It was all different when he was around. He looked after me, I've never been able to look after myself. He'd of looked after the boy too, the day he walked out was the day that led us all to this. I still don't blame him, I can't, he didn't know what to do, he couldn't handle it all, he was scared and he ran, if I had the choice at the time I think I would have ran too. I didn't have that choice though, I had to stay.

I remember looking into his big blue eyes as he lay in my lap. I knew I couldn't leave him, I couldn't give him to no one else. I promised myself that day they I would do the best I could for him, try to give him the best life I possibly could, it ain't really worked out like that, I'm still trying but I'm starting to give up hope that things will ever work out the way I wanted them to. People will probably say it's my own fault, it's because I'm selfish, but I don't know any other way to handle life. I was too young, they don't think about that though do they? They just want to put you down all the time.

There's a couple of kids in the park, not sure what they are doing but it's probably not something good at this time of night. I know some of them are going in there to do gear. When I see them in there I want to shake them, I want to ask them what the fuck do they think they are doing, why are they wasting their lives going down the same fucking road I went down. They probably think it's one of them roads where you can just turn around and walk back, but it ain't, it's nothing like that, it's a long straight road where a brick wall follows right behind you.

The house is quiet, he must have gone to bed because none of the lights are on. I wonder what he does in the evenings? I don't ask because it makes me feel even more guilty. It's always so fucking cold in here, I really must buy us a heater so he can keep warm at night, I meant to buy one last week but I forgot. I sit down at the kitchen table and smoke a cigarette, and another one. I'm starting to feel sick, the goose pimples rising on my skin. I'll wait until I'm in my room though, it feels better when you tease yourself, it's the one rule I have as well, only in my room.

I stand up and look at the small mirror that's on the kitchen wall. My eyes are dark, my face skinny and pale even with make up on I look ill. How must he feel to have this come home to him every single night? I light another cigarette and sit down, I'll take that mirror down in the morning, I don't want to have to keep looking at myself when I get in. One last cigarette before I go and check on him, I have to smoke at least three, I'm nervous, I keep waiting for the day where he isn't there when I get home, that he's had enough and run away.

I look through the crack in the door, he looks asleep but I'm sure he is awake. There's a small smile on his face, he knows that I'm here. I'm feeling a bit shaky so I hold on to the door handle, I don't want to walk away just yet. I can't believe that such a complete waste of a fucking life like me could have created something as beautiful as him. I don't know where he got his intelligence from either, I doubt it was from me, well it can't have been. I kiss my finger tips and blow it towards him, smile and walk to my room, the sickness is coming fast and I need to stop it.

You can like my Facebook Page at

https://www.facebook.com/Seanhoganwriter/

Follow me on Twitter at https://twitter.com/SeanHogan6

You can email me at sean@sdhogan.com

Printed in Great Britain
by Amazon